Legacy

An Anthology

Turn to page 120

velvet morning
press

Published by Velvet Morning Press

Copyright © 2015 Velvet Morning Press

ISBN-13: 978-0692346952
ISBN-10: 0692346953

Cover design by Vicki Lesage and Ellen Meyer

A Note from the Editors

Legacy... So much more than simply the title of this anthology, the mere notion of "legacy" is anchored in our daily lives from our first breath to well beyond our last. Present in our collective memories, it is inevitable.

In this anthology, authors with diverse backgrounds and writing styles share their take on the idea of legacy. The word "legacy" has a heaviness to it, perhaps due to its sense of finality: *This is what you leave behind.* In the tales they weave, our contributors show us that legacy, indeed, can mean sadness, but it can just as easily mean happiness.

Within these pages, there is laughter, pride and hope. There is romance and rock and roll. Certain messages are eerie, while others bestow a sense of peace. The collection, through the discerning lens of each writer, runs the gamut of the human experience. Many of the stories are fiction, and some are nonfiction.

Our *Legacy* authors don't aim to answer a question, but instead, to generate more questions in their own minds and in the minds of the reader. To contemplate, to explore. It is a quest, and as writer and reader, we embark upon it together.

Velvet Morning Press
April 2015

*To readers, for making our words withstand
the test of time*

Table of Contents

Preface
Allison Hiltz

My love of reading started long before I picked up my first book. Both of my parents are readers, and there isn't a time in my life that I can remember not having a book within arm's reach. That said, as much as I attribute my love of books to my parents, I must thank my grandmother for passing on the handy skill of completely tuning out the world when absorbed in a good book. In other words, she taught me the importance of selective hearing.

I can pinpoint two moments in my life that have made me who I am as a reader. When I was six, I stayed home from school sick and read *Charlotte's Web* by E.B. White in one day. I can't say I was as excited at the time about my achievement as I am about it now, but I remember the elation I felt after finishing the story. The second book is *Where the Red Fern Grows* by Wilson Rawls, which I read when I was nine. This one stands alone at the pinnacle of my proverbial book pyramid as "the reason" I am a reader. It was the first book I remember re-reading and is why I have dogs.

Given my insatiable appetite for books, it doesn't surprise many people that I have a book blog. It might, however, surprise them to learn that I had no intention of ever starting one, and, instead, started out blogging about my hip surgeries. As it turns out, there's only so much you can say about that particular topic. So as I recovered in early 2012, I began reviewing books under the influence of some heavy painkillers, accidentally bought a domain and managed to become a book blogger. As I look back on that moment, I think to myself, *Wow, I got lucky!* (but I also think, *My poor husband!*)

I say "lucky" because The Book Wheel (named as such because my world revolves around books and books make the world go round) has had some incredible successes. It won several awards and is now associated with this wonderful anthology you're reading today. It's also allowed me to break into the writing community and make friends with some excellent authors, one of whom sparked the idea for the original #30Authors event. Jenny Milchman (a.k.a. Superstar) asked me last summer to brainstorm how to connect authors and readers in a fun and unique way. Being the overachiever that I am, I came up with the idea for #30Authors: Have 30 authors review their favorite recent read on 30 different blogs. The month-long event was a huge success, and I couldn't have done it without the help of some truly terrific and supportive bloggers and authors.

To make things even more exciting, #30Authors contributor Adria J. Cimino and author Vicki Lesage approached me about turning the event into an anthology via their independent press, Velvet Morning Press. Thus, *Legacy* was born. We chose the theme of "legacy" because it is such an integral part of writing.

Words remain. So why not ask the contributors to explore this theme that is the essence of their craft? We asked each author to imagine him or herself locked away in a castle and to write either a short fiction or nonfiction piece about what legacy means to them.

To keep true to the original goal of #30Authors, which was to connect readers and authors, contributors live-tweeted their writing experiences for one month. During this time, ideas were shared, but more importantly, relationships were built. The ensuing chapters are the culmination of these interconnected, yet independent, writers.

Allison Hiltz
The Book Wheel

The Uraniums
Kristopher Jansma

The Uraniums played just one show before splitting up for good in October of 1963. This was at the infamous 92 Club, a dank pub basement outside of Cambridge, best known in those days for booking folk acts like Dylan and Baez for in-the-know Harvard and BU undergraduates. Fire codes mandated a maximum of 175 persons, but receipts from that night show that 238 ticket stubs were sold and ripped for what would by morning be known as a truly singular experience in Rock and Roll history.

When I say it was *singular* I mean all aspects of this word: uncommon, peculiar, never reproduced. On the powder-blue graph paper of a mathematician, a singularity is a point of *un*-definition. An exceptional set which fails to behave as expected. A seemingly ordinary course of data suddenly "explodes" (their terminology) to plus-or-minus infinity and loses all describable character. This is precisely what Theodorus Hamilton and his cohorts accomplished that night in Boston, in 1963.

But think also of the impossibly empty universe of the astronomer, whose "singularity" refers to a black hole—a point with no volume and infinite density, where all matter is obliterated by limitless gravity. These words could also apply to the vibrations of Sarah Dickens' mandolin, and to the guitars of Roger Barnacle and Jackson Press. If it could have been recreated, we will never know. All we know is that it was not. By morning the nine members of The Uraniums would all go their separate ways.

What's even more startling though, is that The Uraniums had never played all together before that night either. As a ninesome, no one quite anticipated what the results would be. The only time keyboardist S.L. Miles showed up to the early sessions, accordion player Penny Orbach was being held for questioning by the Boston Police in connection with graffiti that had cropped up over in Chinatown. By the time she was released, Miles had been forced out of town by a family emergency. The result being that even the nine members of The Uraniums had no expectation that the history of rock music would be irreversibly altered on that evening in 1963. Indeed, absolutely no one expected much of anything, which is why, tragically, no recordings were even made. The Uraniums had spoken about the gig at the 92 Club as little more than a toe-in-the-water, just a rehearsal for a bigger show a month later at the nearby Watertown Community Center—which would, for various complicated reasons, never happen. As I've said, the 92 Club show would be their only performance and were it not for the 238 witnesses (myself included) the impact of The Uraniums would have fizzled into nothingness.

Theodorus Hamilton was, ostensibly, the founder of

the nontet. He penned the lyrics to the songs they sang that night and led the improvisation of several additional songs when the band soon ran out of material. Instrumentally, however, his role was always relatively background. A mercurial demon on the flute, a satanic wizard on the tambourine and triangle, Theodorus was by day a Harvard Divinity student with a penchant for rabble-rousing.

He'd held his first rally about 10 minutes into the first day of classes, in fervent protest of the school cafeteria's mass-produced strawberry jam. He marched around to the neighboring tables, sampling each of their jams. Finding them all to be distasteful, he rose up onto the central table and raised the rancid jam toward God, to whom he declared it to be an offense. He had such a presence, such a way with words, that soon 200 other breakfasting students rose to their own tabletops, and 14 members of the serving staff jumped ship as well. Theodorus then led the students in a rowdy smashing of the offending jars and marched off across the campus and into a community garden in Cambridge, where fresh strawberries turned out not to be available, and so they instead had plums.

All this to say he was quite notorious already by the start of his junior year, and so when Theodorus began asking around about forming a band, large numbers of Harvard students, locals and friends from sister schools turned out for the audition.

His perfectionism at first threatened the whole enterprise. Theodorus rejected dozens of singers, violinists, drummers and saxophone players. It was not until the second day that he discovered mandolin player Sarah Dickens, who'd traveled out from Amherst for the occasion. A slim and severe girl with a caustic attitude, Sarah had grated on Theodorus from the first moment. She wore all black with a high-buttoned collar, and she kept her mouth covered with her hand, even while speaking.

"Do you have the flu?" he'd asked.

"No!" she'd cried, as if she hadn't even *considered* the flu until then. "Do you?"

But when she finally lowered her hands to play, Theodorus was moved to distraction by both her quietly ferocious music and her hieroglyphic smile—and their brief (and reputedly chaste) love affair began that afternoon in a cloakroom at the Theological Library. After that day, they were rarely seen more than a hair's breadth apart, and together they formed the gray, shale heart of The Uraniums—hard, gleaming and certain to splinter.

The other seven members of the band were introduced steadily over the subsequent weeks.

Bass player Ernesto Valdez sent an audition tape from Italy, where he was studying abroad at the time—getting dual degrees in figurative painting and alcoholic consumption. News of The Uraniums had reached him by wire and Valdez never hesitated once he heard Theodorus was involved. Upon news of his acceptance, Valdez hopped a flight back to Boston, leaving the Tuscan Hills thundering with the echoes of 10 or 12 breaking hearts.

S.L. Miles, on keyboard, was found trolling around Boston Commons wearing an ill-fitting aviator's cap, bragging to any who would listen that he was the greatest pianist since Thelonious Monk. Miles had quit school, and then the Army, and finally the family artichoke-bottling business. I used to see him out there, sometimes. He'd sit with his keyboard, never playing, taking quarters when they were dropped but never begging, always bragging. When anyone told him to put his money where his mouth was, he told them they just didn't *get* it. But when Theodorus told him to, Miles played, and Miles was in.

Then came Nelly Finch, whose birdsong lilting was enough to overcome even the "Goldwater for President" button she'd pinned neatly to her blouse. She was all Southern brass and charm.

Theodorus once remarked, "If you try to hate her, she'll tell you nicely you're wrong, and then suddenly you'll see that you are."

Her friend, the goofy, buck-toothed Penny Orbach, was the only accordion player to try out and so she was a shoo-in—despite placing whoopee cushions on Theodorus' chair and drawing "Kilroy Was Here" doodles all over the lyric sheets while he'd been dealing with Nelly. When the two ladies left, all that could be said for sure was that *one* of them had poured a pound of macaroni salad into the heating duct in the bathroom.

Theodorus was content to leave it at that—six musicians seemed like plenty—but then Roger Barnacle, Jackson Press and Henry Kobayashi came in as a set. They were the remnants of a progressive rock band that had lost its lead guitarist and lyricist, Hughley Howard, to an automobile accident on the Mass Pike earlier that year. An ACME produce truck had taken out the poor boy's motorcycle and sent him flying a hundred yards into a utility pole. Barnacle and Press each played guitar with an abandon that could be called unparalleled if there hadn't been two of them. All either of them would say about Kobayashi, the drummer, was that he was brilliant, spoke no English and was very, very weird.

What can be said about the show itself?

There are facts: that it was over five hours in length; that they played *Seferis in the Jungle*, *Flying Scotsman*, *705*, *No Newspapers* and *Come Down Joe Walker*, along with dozens of other songs whose titles were unclear—several of which had no proper titles, since they were improvised on the spot; that they started out wearing Baptist choir robes on Theodorus' insistence (to show solidarity with the Birmingham church bombings) but that these were soon torn off; that they covered *I Fall to Pieces* by the recently departed Patsy Cline; that they performed one number consisting only of Orbach reading off the names of nuclear submariners that had drowned; that S.L. Miles introduced himself as an understudy on *General Hospital*. These facts are verifiable, but they cannot begin to sum up the greatness of that night.

There are impressions: that Barnacle's experimentation with echoes that night was bold and revolutionary; that Finch's mocking tone set an unanticipated wryness to the somber lyrics of Theodorus; that Sarah Dickens' mandolin playing was eerily prescient of what would come on later Zeppelin tracks; that S.L. Miles played with the loving fearlessness of a child—tinkering with keys that so-called "experienced" players had lost track of; that Jackson Press sang better than he ever would in his lengthy later career. These impressions are subjective, but I can assure you none are too far from the mark.

There are myths: that Ernesto Valdez drank six bottles of Pernod over the course of the night; that Penny Orbach smashed her accordion to pieces after the third hour and fashioned the ripped bellows into a cape; that Kobayashi completely bugged out in the middle of *Volcanic Interruptions*, dove off the stage, disappeared for several minutes and returned with a watermelon under each arm; that Theodorus Hamilton burned an effigy of then Harvard President Nathan M. Pusey; that the entire show only ended in the fifth hour because a paramilitary police team broke down the barricaded door, and that as a result, all 238 audience members in attendance were placed onto an FBI watch list. These myths are absurd, though perhaps none are without their charms.

Once the show ended, around three in the morning, the nine musicians deliriously disassembled their equipment and parted ways—all apparently eager to rejoin to practice for next month's Watertown Community Center show. Each of them knew they had accomplished something unknown and undefinable that night, and yet they were eager to get away from one another, perhaps because with the lights up and the crowd cleared, they did not quite believe it had happened themselves. And within a week they had all left Cambridge—some disappeared almost as quickly as they were able.

As near as anyone could tell this was not a coordinated exodus. In fact, the few members of the band who have spoken publicly about the incident have all said they left without a word to the others and had no idea the other eight would not go on to Watertown with some replacement.

Theodorus Hamilton took off that very night, with his flute and his tambourine and his triangle and nothing else. He marched south over the Charles River and 20 miles down Blue Hill Avenue, finding himself at Ponkapoag Pond, where he remained for several years in relative solitude, bothered only by the occasional sliced ball from the adjacent Ponkapoag Golf & Country Club.

On the subject of *why* he went to the pond, Theodorus Hamilton eventually wrote a lengthy account of his days there, called simply *Ponkapoag*, in which he spoke of the simple pleasures of fishing and bathing nude in the pond—of the thrill of hiding in the tops of a tall tree while being pursued by angry country club groundskeepers. It is a spiritual book, and he makes no mention of The Uraniums at all—but writes instead about the delicacy of birds' eggs, the sturdiness of reeds and the wily nature of the Massachusetts fox. Of music he wrote only of the serenading of loons, the buzzing of flies in spiders' webs and the screeching of owls that wished they had never been born into this world. When he returned to city life a few years later, he discovered Kennedy had been shot, the Army draft board had been looking for him, China had developed a hydrogen bomb, and Nixon was on his way to being elected. Theodorus turned right around, tired and tubercular, and started hitching west toward the Great Lakes, with his eye on Canada and then Alaska beyond.

Many speculate his reason for leaving was somehow linked to Sarah Dickens, and that the two must have fought at the 92 Club that night and ended their relationship just after the show. Though I have no proof besides what I saw that night between them on stage, I suspect the raw energy of that epic performance ignited something in both band members that, in the ringing silence of the post-show fallout, neither could quite release. Germ-phobic Dickens was oil to the water of Hamilton's divine countenance. Lines of great force had been pushed through the bedrock and when the particulate bonds began to break, the result was an explosive silence. Sarah Dickens returned to Amherst via the 7:17 train that morning and went to her parents' home. She did not emerge for 20 years, and then only because her pallbearers were carrying her out to the cemetery.

In the intervening time, she communicated often, through letters to some of the other band members, asking if anyone knew where Theodorus was. Copies of these letters were located upon her death by Sarah's sisters, in a chest filled with 1,132 compositions for the mandolin—though she had not played a note since the night with The Uraniums. Her dust-coated instrument, indeed, had been sitting 10 feet from her desk on a shelf in the attic room—with frayed strings—un-tuned and untouched for 20 years.

Ernesto Valdez fled to France where he fell in with a generation of lost musicians from the States, who together drank themselves to pieces under Parisian and Madridian moons. His simple, straightforward playing later spurred a hundred lesser imitators. Before long he became something of a national treasure, though he spent the better part of his career anywhere but America and reportedly fell in with socialists. He took up hunting in the hinterlands of Africa and fishing in the deep blue trenches off of Vieques. He married and divorced, married and divorced, married and divorced, married and blew his head off with an elephant gun just before his 50th birthday.

Three days after the 92 Club show, S.L. Miles stumbled onto *Advaita Vedanta*, a sub-sect of Zen Buddhism that was steadily taking hold of the Harvard undergraduates who frequented the Commons at the time. Miles fancied himself every bit as easily taken-in as any Harvard student, and so he was. He continued to play the keyboard, but rarely granted interviews and did not speak about The Uraniums' show. Instead, he kept trying to redirect fans to his newer compositions, which were more Eastern-influenced—less tightly constructed and wider sweeping. Many fans were unimpressed by this shift. In fact, several spoke scathingly of him afterwards—upset they'd ever been swayed by his music. Many swore to anyone who would listen that their interest in Miles had only been an understandable folly of youth. They saw his act now as juvenile and *minor*. Miles soon skipped town and headed out toward the woods, perhaps inspired by the earlier flight of Theodorus, remaining there until his recent death. Generations of listeners still wait to learn if he continued to compose in his reclusion.

Nelly Finch turned down the calls of agents and producers following the 92 Club show. Some believe she was devastated by Goldwater's defeat to Johnson in '64. Others said the Summer of Love was just too much for her. We do know that, for some time, she and Penny Orbach were very close and rumored to be working together on an album, but when Penny's work emerged steadily in the later decades there was no evidence of Finch on any of the tracks. Many said Finch and Orbach were lovers; many said they were bad drunks. Whatever the case, Orbach's seminal albums for the accordion were certainly impressive feats of musicianship: paranoidly blending epic richness with commercial jingling, and inspiring an entire generation of genius accordionists to follow. Both women live today, but neither is heard from. While Finch supposedly lives in Alabama with her older sister and refuses to give interviews, Orbach resides in Manhattan in complete anonymity. There are those in the Village who claim to have seen her—an older woman with buck teeth who no one seems to know, smoking dope at a record release party or spray-painting cartoonish accordions onto the brick walls of the tenement houses.

These figures all remained alive mainly in the gossip and imagination of the world's musical elite. The final three members of The Uraniums—Roger Barnacle, Jackson Press and Henry Kobayashi—each became household names, though in extremely different ways, each occupying, in his own way, one of the subsequent decades of the twentieth century.

Roger Barnacle left the show that night and met some fans on the Weeks Bridge. They took some acid off some pink elephant stamps and the old Barnacle was scraped off, so to speak. Great madness gripped him in its Technicolor tentacles. He spacily unwound all the strings on his guitar and dreamily wove them into the hair of a young woman who thought she was a bird's nest. He ate a third of his left shoe and streaked up Massachusetts Avenue, setting mailboxes on fire as they left the city. Twelve hours later, psychedelic playtime over, they stumbled to a nearby barn to rest in a hayloft. The fans awoke the next day to find Roger Barnacle, still quite berserk, singing selections from *My Fair Lady* to an immense, black pig.

Barnacle vanished. Fans fed rumors he was in an asylum somewhere, on a permanent bad trip after doing a whole blotter of acid in one sitting. They said he was, now, forever convinced he was a teapot—wandering about the padded rooms attempting to pour himself out for people. The perhaps sadder truth is he moved home with his mother and sister, took up vegetable gardening and bicycling, and lived a relatively quiet life before dying of cancer in his old and feeble age.

No doubt you today know at least a dozen Jackson Press songs. His first solo album, *Piping Hot Off the Wall*, rocketed him to instant fame. A natural pop songwriter, his R&B sensibility played well in the roiling cultural Charybdis that was the 1970s, and then evolved with the times and technologies that came after, remaining an international force to be reckoned with, well into the twenty-first century. Press recorded one platinum album after the next. He toured the world, making billions, meeting prime ministers and presidents and playing the Super Bowl. People in Myanmar and Dubai and Siberia and Tierra del Fuego knew his songs: *Mirror Man* and *Corrupt* and *Jeanie G.* and *White Knuckle* and *Get Going* and *Dark or Light*. It was a given that he would win a Grammy any year he put out an album. He got involved in international charities, trying to use his fame to combat starvation and malaria, and provide potable water to villages. The name of Jackson Press went down in Rock history alongside Elvis and Lennon, but only his most fervent fans knew he had once been a member of The Uraniums—just a brief blip in the immense, mega, titanic, interstellar career that had followed.

And oh, yes, there were questions—many questions—about the hair plugs and the water park he lived in and the little girls and the high-profile abuse trials and the off-kilter marriages and his oddly named children. But his fame was too deep, too wide and too vast to be drained away by any of these oddities. His was the sort of fervent, self-propelling fame that no one— least of all Press himself—could do anything to stop. When he eventually overdosed on painkillers, the world took a holiday. His name and face filled every television screen on every channel for half a week. Emperors and kings had had smaller funerals. A year earlier, Barnacle had died peacefully at home, barely remembered by anyone.

So. What of Henry Kobayashi? Of him, the last, we know the least, which perhaps is just as well. He disappeared more completely than the rest and to this day has not been seen. Some say he changed his name and went back to teaching mathematics, which he had earned his PhD in before the show, at the young age of 22. Some say he defected to North Korea and he is the (perhaps unwilling) architect of their nuclear strategies. Others say he walked off into the Nevada desert with no intentions of surviving. Still others say he is the one behind a string of pipe-bomb attacks that have spanned 30 years, directed at various university professors, military and airline targets. Bits and pieces of wood consistent with drumsticks have been found, according to the FBI, amidst the shrapnel in several of the devices.

I really can't say one way or the other. I'm not him, you see—I'm not anybody. I was just there. I just saw it all that night and felt myself, like those nine, irrevocably altered by that performance. By a conflagration of immense talents that could not ever be reproduced. Even if the Watertown Community Center show had been held as scheduled, it could not have been the same. Perhaps it is better anyway, that those notes resonate now only in our memories. They are in there. Trapped in pulpy nets of dendritic bridges, synaptic threads that, even then, were being stripped of their sheaths by tendrils of marijuana smoke and warm beer, by innocuous tabs of LSD-25, by ghostly amphetiminic and barbitutive winds. Forty years later, those precious cells have endured fourteen hundred further days of fractured and steady dying, of triumphant and orgasmic living. Of day after day of our records being overwritten by lesser and lesser moments. It ought to be forgotten, just a bit of static and fuzz in the minds of 238 erstwhile Bostonians and the nine Uraniums—though most are dead and the remainder are ghosts regardless. But I can tell you. I was there. I cannot forget it. What took place there that night was nuclear. We were all taken apart on a molecular level, and our unstable atoms were rearranged. We were weaponized and miniaturized. It is still in here somewhere, waiting to go off.

The Monument
Marissa Stapley

The town hasn't changed much, and Delia can't
figure out if this is what she'd hoped. She supposes it was
part of the reason she and Anthony had been so charmed
by it in the first place, all those years ago. They had
found the town peculiar, but in a good way—and she
probably still would, if she were in the mood to be
charitable. But Delia is not, and never will be again, when
it comes to this particular town. Even the name—
Gananoque—is irritating to her. The memory of the way
the townspeople called it "Gan," as though it were a
family member, or a dear old friend, or they were in a
club that only the people who lived there year-round got
to be in.

Arriving back in Gan (Delia calls it that in her mind
too, and then hates herself for it, the way she might hate
herself for inadvertently referring to her ex-husband by
the pet name his lover called him, for example) is like
being hit with a blunt object. When she drives through
the archway that says, "Welcome to Gananoque," she

slows the car and rubs the side of her head. She considers making a U-turn and driving all the way back to Ithaca. But she doesn't. She presses her foot on the gas and continues driving to the Holiday Inn Express, where she has booked a room because there is nowhere else to stay at this time of year. The girl at the check-in desk tells her the continental breakfast is "not to be missed." Apparently, there is something called a pancake machine. "We just got it," the girl, who has straight but yellowed teeth, says. "You just push a button and out comes a pancake."

"How exciting," Delia says, but the girl either ignores or does not grasp the sarcasm. Upstairs, Delia puts her valise on the bed but does not open it. Instead, she keeps her coat on, hoists her purse higher on her shoulder and leaves the room. She drives into town again and finds a parking spot. The piles of snow banked up beside the curbs make the sidewalks look like little tunnels. They had never been there in winter, she and Anthony. Only summer. So *this* is different at least, this snowy shroud the town is enveloped in. It helps dull the memories somewhat, and she is grateful for it. Or perhaps grateful is not the right word.

Why have I come?

She has thought about returning, so many times, over the years. But she did not come for her son's funeral—she has regretted this, always—so why *now*? She can't answer this. What she hopes to accomplish by coming never crystallized in her mind during the planning of the trip, or the hours she spent driving there, as she had hoped it would. And so she struggles as she stands on the sidewalk to come up with a reason not to get into her car and drive away, back through the arches. *I could just go. Right now.* She won't even stop at the hotel to pick up her valise or check out. She'll toss her room key out the window as she drives, feel for a moment like a criminal on the run. She'll replace the luggage, the clothing and toiletries in the valise once she's back in Ithaca. Or maybe she won't. She has too much stuff anyway. She finds herself strangely elated by the idea of driving, unencumbered, out onto the highway again. Over the border and home. Safe.

But lonely.

This is the answer. This is why she has come. Because she is so alone that even one glimpse of the girl has the potential to provide solace. Because it has taken her this long to realize that, and it is too late now, but she still has to see.

After Chase died, she and Anthony's marriage did not last long. Delia had read a study somewhere about the percentage of marriages that failed once a child was lost or tragedy struck, and she felt relief in using this as an excuse to dissolve it. She was not ostracized by her friends the way some women were when they left their husbands. He didn't even seem to resent her that much, though he pretended to be angry. Anthony was and always had been a blustering, angry man, used to getting what he wanted—and when he didn't, look out. She remembers getting the news about Chase and being on one hand torn apart by her grief. And on the other, terrified of the rage she knew Anthony would fly into. Though she *had* been surprised with how quickly it had flamed out. How swiftly it had deadened him, inside and out. She wonders if she would have stayed with him, had he been able to sustain the rage longer, perhaps pass some of it along to her, goad her into anger instead of anguish.

But that was a long time ago. 1967. Back then, she had believed that perhaps she could move on from the loss of her son—upon whom both she and Anthony had pinned a variety of hopes and dreams, different to each of them, and had never thought to check in with him, with *Chase*, about what *he* wanted—and build a new life.

Delia had gone through anger, yes, a brief anger that was one of the stages of grief—at least, that's what the self-help books had told her—and had raged inwardly against her son. *How could you be so bloody irresponsible? Why would you go out on the river on the early ice with your young wife? Why would you take a risk like that, when you had a baby at home?* But she knew why. He was following his passion, building his dream, working frantically to construct the fishing camp with his wife before the season was over. And she had raised him to believe in himself—so, likely, he had believed himself to be invincible. *My fault, in the end.*

When she had moved through the anger phase, she had even felt a grudging admiration for him. Had *she* ever followed a passion? No, never. And now she is an 80-year-old woman who is estranged from the rest of her children for committing various offenses—chiding a grandchild for his lamentable manners here, making a cruel comment about one of her daughters' husbands there, withholding affection when they were young, apparently, all of them had told her this—and trailing behind her not one but two unsuccessful marriages. And all the second marriage got her was a smattering of stepchildren to resent her and excommunicate her, too. She can't even remember why. She supposes she could laugh about it, if it weren't so pitiful.

She walks carefully along the slushy sidewalk. Is she looking for the girl? Possibly, yes. (Of course she is; why else would she be there?) *The girl.* This is how she has always referred to Chase's child in her mind. A distant pronoun—and certainly not as her granddaughter, no, never that. She walks down Main Street and turns right, left, left, until she can see the river and the old, long-closed factories, as well as the row of hotels and inns that are open in summer but are not open now.

Soon, as she knew she would be, she is standing in front of Summers' Inn, the place where Virginia—who had captured her son's heart and caused him to abdicate the family throne and move to this town to become a muskellunge fishing guide, of all things—was raised, the place they came to as a family once, for a vacation that would change the course of their lives forever.

The inn is perched at the edge of the riverbank, at the point where the Gananoque River flows into the St. Lawrence and loses its identity completely. Delia sees the yellow-gray stone walls of the inn, the navy blue shutters on every window, the red roof, the weathervane in the shape of a sturgeon. She sees the guest cabins and the dock and the white-painted boathouse and the old gas pump. She sees the tree with the rope hanging from it, and then, suddenly, it is no longer winter, and there is sun shining through pine boughs, and the wooden window boxes are filled with white zinnia and ivy, and Chase is swinging out over the river on the rope tied to the maple tree, and there are deck chairs and the soft murmur of conversation and music and Delia is crying. Quickly, she wipes the tears away.

The front door of the inn opens. Without looking to see who it is, Delia moves off, rushes down the street, does not walk carefully now, does not worry about slipping and falling and breaking her hip, and instead focuses on her flight away from that place. She doesn't get far, because she is too old to move very fast. She only makes it to the end of the street before she is breathless. She stops and looks back and sees a young woman in a white parka shoveling the front steps. *The girl.* Delia knows.

She watches as the girl works, then leans the shovel against the outer wall of the inn and drags a container out from under the stairs and begins to shake salt onto the walk. The dutiful granddaughter, caring for Lilly and

George, who would have raised her after both her parents died that night on the ice. Delia is filled with impotent jealousy. She is sure the girl will look up, alerted to her presence by the power of her bad feelings, but the girl is absorbed in what she's doing and does not. *Safe. You are safe. Keep walking.* But Delia can't move. There is a blond braid poking out from beneath the girl's woolen hat. Delia can't see her face, because she is too far away and she is not wearing her glasses.

Soon, too soon—because Delia, despite herself, is drinking in the girl's presence, hungrily, fearfully—the girl replaces the container under the steps. She claps her mittened hands together, turns and starts down the walkway. She crosses the street and walks toward Delia while Delia stands still, too frightened to move. *Go! Turn around!* But then the girl crosses the street. Delia watches as she turns into the parking lot of the play house, where in the summer a theater company puts on plays and musicals for the tourists. *We had watched* The King and I *there. We had seen* On Golden Pond.

Delia begins to move, so she can keep the girl in her sights. The girl is standing at the side door of the play house now, removing her mittens, reaching into her pocket, producing a key. It is at this point that she finally looks up, finally senses she is being observed. She raises a hand and waves in that small town way people who live in small towns wave, as if everyone is a friend. And Delia finds herself waving back—and in that moment, the loneliness retreats. Then the girl opens the door and goes inside the play house.

Delia retraces her path, back the way she has come, right, right, left this time and back onto Main. She feels strangely exhilarated, in a way she hasn't in a long time. She walks until she reaches a café. Inside, she orders a pot of tea and then, impulsively, a maple scone. People come in and out. Everyone seems to know everyone else, and many people give her the same casual wave the girl had.

Delia bites into the scone—it is crumbly and cakey, there is icing on it, it reminds her of something from her childhood—and allows herself to imagine what it might be like to live in a place like this. Too soon, though, the scone is gone, and her tea is tepid. She checks her watch. An hour has passed. She does not know what to do with herself, but feels she cannot loiter any longer. Outside, she walks back the way she came once more, down the streets that are suddenly as familiar as home, but painfully so. She goes to the play house. She tries the door. It is locked, of course. *What on earth are you doing?*

She peers inside at the darkness and thinks the girl must not be there any more, but then she sees her, passing by with a sheaf of papers. Delia ducks, and the movement alerts the girl to her presence. The girl stops, startled, and then she laughs and goes to the door, unlocks it and pokes her head out.

"You scared me," she says, laughing again. "For a minute, with that coat, I thought you were—I don't know, a *bear* or something." She stops laughing when she seems to realize Delia is not laughing, not even smiling.

There is an uncomfortable silence during which time Delia looks at the girl's face and tries not to appear as desperately ravenous as she is. But there is nothing in the girl's face to feed her hunger. The girl is a dead ringer for her mother, Virginia. But she does not look like Chase at all, and, realizing this, Delia feels herself harden against the girl. She knows with sudden clarity that the moment when she allowed herself to wave and felt her desolation temporarily recoil is all she's going to get.

"Is there something I can help you with?" *Mae. Her name is Mae.*

"I was wondering if there are any plays scheduled. I'm just here for a day or two, and I thought I might…"

"You're in luck. Tomorrow there's a matinee. It's just community theater, so not quite, or anywhere near, as professional as what you might see here in the summer, but it's not bad, if I do say so myself. I'm in it," she continues, and Delia thinks she senses something nervous in the girl's chatter. Or maybe it's just the way she is when she talks to strangers, or when she talks at all. What does Delia know about this girl? "Romeo and Juliet. We've condensed it from the original version. So it's shorter."

"That's generally what happens when one condenses something," Delia says dryly, and then, with further clarity, she knows why her daughters don't want anything to do with her. She remembers one of them saying once, "Why do you always have to be so mean?" She doesn't intend it, not really. But she *is* mean.

The girl seems immune to it, though. "Yes, true," she says. "My Aunt Viv is the one who did it, and she told me she didn't want to have to cut *anything*. I mean, it's Shakespeare, who does? But really, on a Sunday afternoon, in a cold theater, no one has the time or inclination to sit through the full version of anything. I'm not making it sound that attractive, am I? I'm probably driving you away."

"No, not at all. I'll be there. What time?"

"Two-thirty tomorrow. You can get your ticket at the door."

"See you then," Delia says, and she retraces her steps for the final time that day, finds her car, drives back to the hotel, enters her room, lies down on her bed and falls asleep blanketed by her coat.

Delia parks in the lot of the play house. She is early, so she waits in the car, the key still in the ignition, the heat still on, until five minutes before the show is scheduled to begin. Inside, she buys a ticket from a young man sitting at a table. Ten dollars. The boy has trouble making change from Delia's 50-dollar bill. "Don't worry," Delia says. "Just keep it." On a sign, it says the show is a fundraiser for a local organization that raises money for the underprivileged youth in town to engage in the arts. Art lessons, music lessons, dance classes. *Why bother*, Delia thinks, and knows this is another of her cruel thoughts.

Delia finds a seat near the back. The play begins almost the moment her back hits the seat.

From forth the fatal loins of these two foes. A pair of star-cross'd lovers take their life.

She feels bored, as she always does when watching live theater. Until the girl comes out. It surprises her that the girl is not playing Juliet, as she had expected. She is Lady Capulet. *This is because she's not a girl*, Delia reminds herself. *She is in her twenties.* The girl who plays Juliet is *truly* a girl, probably no more than 16.

Delia finds her attention wandering when Mae is not on stage, but focuses hard every time she appears. She is a surprisingly good actress. She is better than the young girl playing Juliet, for example, who is passionate, yes, but who is also obviously *acting*, who does not necessarily have an understanding of the words she speaks. Whereas Mae speaks the words easily and causes them to make sense because she seems to see the sense *in* them. The pain in them. The pain that a mother would feel as she loses her child in slow increments.

"Is there no pity sitting in the clouds, that sees to the bottom of my grief?" the girl playing Juliet shouts, clasping her hands together at her pale bosom. "O sweet my mother, cast me not away! Delay this marriage for a month, a week; or, if you do not, make the bridal bed in that dim monument where Tybalt lies."

In that dim monument.

Delia finds herself watching Mae even more closely now, finds her own heart pounding as this young woman, her granddaughter, *there*, she has uttered the words, even inwardly, says: "Talk not to me, for I'll not speak a word: Do as thou wilt, for I have done with thee."

For I have done with thee.

Delia stands and leaves the theater. She goes into the restroom. She thinks she might leave, but in the end she does not. She washes her hands in order to justify her trip to the restroom, and then returns to the theater and sees the play through to the end, winces but stays in her seat when her granddaughter as Lady Capulet shouts, "O me, O me! My child, my only life, Revive, look up, or I will die with thee! Help, help! Call help."

Yes, she thinks. *Yes. Or I will die with thee.* This is exactly what it feels like.

And later:

"This sight of death is as a bell, that warns my old age to a sepulchre." She understands that too. The death of her son had shriveled her, and there it is. The end. *Finis.*

The curtain goes down and then it rises upon the members of the cast, who are now smiling and holding hands. Romeo and Juliet are now risen from the dead and bowing. An old man in the front row stands and is presenting Mae with a small bouquet of tulips wrapped in colored cellophane and he, Delia realizes, is the grandfather. The father of Virginia. And there is the grandmother, there is Lilly, beaming and kissing her granddaughter's cheek. Delia turns away because she hates them for having had for so long what she does not, and never will.

The patrons are moving into the lobby area, where there is a small bar with wine for sale. Delia surprises herself by buying a glass. It is terrible; it tastes like the inside of an apple juice tin.

The conversation rises around her, and Delia stands

there, her fur coat making her uncomfortably hot. Sweat trickles down her back. She looks out at the banks of snow and imagines herself stripping off the jacket and flinging it into a snow bank, then coming back in and speaking to the girl. She gets the same feeling she had in the café, when she was imagining what it would be like to live in a place like Gananoque.

Impossible. Because Delia knows there is no chance the girl will love her, let alone *like* her. That once the townspeople realize who she is, no one will want to be her friend. The casual waves will stop. The bleakness will advance again. Because this girl, this Mae, is not hers. She looks nothing like her son. She is a stranger. Delia looks at her from across the room one last time, just to be certain, but it's true, all of it.

She turns and leaves the play house. The cold air is a relief. She does not drive out of town and fling her key but instead goes to get her bag at the hotel, as she always would have. She leaves the key on the dresser, tells the girl at the desk she is leaving but they can charge her for the night, of course.

"Of course," the girl says, smiling her vacant smile.

"I didn't get to try the pancake machine," Delia finds herself saying. "I overslept this morning."

"Then you should just stay." She is suddenly animated. "It's *really* a can't-miss."

"I have to go," Delia says. "I have a family engagement." This is a lie, but it feels good. She should do this more often, pretend to other people who don't matter to her at all that she is more than what she is. Perhaps she could derive a bit of pleasure from *that*.

It has started to snow, and her car, a Jaguar, is lightly dusted. She gets in the car and takes off her jacket. She folds it and places it in the passenger seat, where it looks like a dead animal. She thinks about how Mae told her she thought she was a bear, and how she laughed. She knows she will never wear that jacket, not ever again.

Back in Ithaca, after a few days have passed, Delia telephones the mayor of Gananoque, and she tells him what she wants. She wants it to be erected anonymously, she tells him. She is a patron of the arts, she says, but she does not like to draw attention to herself. Yes, she *so* enjoyed the play.

And she did, it's true. Especially the part where Montague said, "For I shall raise her statue in pure gold." It gave her the idea. She wants a statue, she says to the mayor, of a young man and a young woman, somewhere near the river, holding hands. And because there is truly nothing, or at least *almost* nothing that money cannot buy (happiness; it's true, it can't buy that, and Delia knows this more than anyone), Delia is eventually assured that the statue will be raised.

It is some comfort to her, in the years that follow, to know it is there. A dim monument, but a monument no less. A testament to her suffering, evidence of her grief, a shrine to the fact that she felt something, once.

Letters of the Night (Adeline and Augustin)
Didier Quémener

The following is presented as a work of fiction. Only the authors of this nighttime correspondence may determine its veracity. Adeline and Augustin share a love story. A story of youth. The creation of an immutable bond between these two characters before the rules of society and adulthood could make their mark. Their reunion, at the castle of Madame de M. during the winter of 1875, is the perfect moment to reignite their passion. The letters of Adeline and Augustin are offered to you exactly as they were found, without a single modification.

Letter I
To Adeline

Dear Adeline,
  Please forgive me for my audacity, sending this letter to you at such a late hour, but I have found it impossible to sleep. Your presence at the castle this evening far

outshone the ostentatiousness of the ball and the company of the other guests.

I found myself riveted to the spot the moment my gaze met yours. Without a doubt, when admiring the young woman you have become, I rediscovered the child I knew from my visits to your family home. However, time seemed to mock me when in your eyes I saw the reflection of those summer games we would play in the park behind your parents' residence, and at the same moment, the charm and elegance that accompany you today. The years that have passed, without your path crossing mine, have graced you with such beauty. If Madame de M. had not introduced us, certainly several more years would have flown by before our lives could touch once again. What a pleasure to have seen you, to have enjoyed your company! If fatigue has not overcome you, a response would culminate this joyful reunion…

Letter II
To Augustin

Dear Augustin,

All is forgiven, for I, too, was not sleeping. As I look back at my memories of you, feisty young man that you were, I suppose I could not expect any less. On the contrary, silence from you certainly would have surprised me. The pleasure to meet again was mine as well, Augustin. You have matured quite a bit after the years abroad, haven't you? You seem to be a man of the world, intelligent, and with a confidence that draws everyone to your side, hoping to share in conversation. Bravo! And I could not help but notice the particular effect you had upon the ladies…

Letter III
To Adeline

Adeline,

I thank you for your words. You are right—my voyages brought me a great deal, intellectually as well as emotionally. And of course the time that passes inexorably leaves its mark, as does the ink on these letters I address to you. Did you know that I have preciously guarded the letters you sent to me during the winters you spent in Italy with your parents? When a sense of melancholy knocks at the doors of my heart, I reread them, one after the other... Do you still have mine?

Letter IIII
To Augustin

I believe your letters are still at our winter residence, but due to the occupation of Rome, my parents recently took flight for Florence. It is possible they have already arrived. The former capital has become so politically unstable that my father decided his only choice was to abandon the family home. It is sad, Augustin. I have the feeling that a part of myself will die the day I learn of its new ownership. But that is life, I suppose. Things change, and we change with them...

Letter V
To Adeline

Life is only worth living, Adeline, if we fear losing it. If the irreplaceable disappears, what is the use of going on? What good is an existence stripped of its principal meaning? The idea of losing the slightest detail fastening my life to yours makes my blood run cold. I dare not think of it! I will buy the house from your parents and contact my friend the Ambassador of France so that he will take the necessary measures to assure its security. Time is ours, so that we may make our mark, so that our memories may take root forever.

Letter VI
To Augustin

Augustin, that is most noble and honorable, and I am grateful. I will let my father know of your intentions, and he certainly will contact you. But tell me, your success seems remarkable. We did not have the opportunity to speak of it during the party, but please share the story of your work. Have you followed in the footsteps of your late grandfather? The business of precious metals appears to be more prolific than ever before.

Letter VII
To Adeline

Business is business. The relations between my father and me, as you knew them, slowly deteriorated following my departure and travels around the world. He always refused to understand my desire for freedom, which makes me think that the example of his life, in a way, served as a point of reference for me. At any cost, I wanted to distance myself from the financial trap in which he found himself ensnared more and more tightly each day. That is why, from my earliest memories, I had this longing to leave, to flee this life of slavery in gold chains, to flee this incessant pressure that eats away at one like an invisible illness.

I am a self-made man, Adeline. I built everything I have little by little, through my travels and encounters. This experience, far from the mundane life you and I have known since our youngest age, was the best of these past years. I encountered people without possessions, whose only riches were fulfilling the daily necessity: survival. I met families whose children started to work at the very moment they had enough strength to stand. I saw misery, Adeline, poverty at its most extreme. I saw the sadness of faces on which time, each day, etches another line as a testament to the suffering.

Do not rely on the futile appearances of a few hours ago. All of that is simply a game of fools. I am not ashamed. I have no remorse for being a part of their world, no regrets about using the situation to my advantage. The truth, Adeline, is that your memory of the Augustin you knew should remain a memory amongst many others. I have liberty, and I choose my destiny, unlike my father. Adulthood has at least given me the opportunity to break free, and independence is priceless.

Letter VIII
To Augustin

My dear Augustin,

Your story is as remarkable as it is poignant. Who would have imagined such adventures? All the same, I was far from guessing you might resent the background that shaped you. What is left of our childhood sentiments? A bittersweet feeling that on one hand draws you to me, yet on the other, distances you irrevocably to the point of disdain for our social class? This class that gave birth to you. Seeking to renounce a part of one's past or abandoning one's origins, in my opinion, is not a mere statement of facts, but rather, the signal of a profound problem. You are perhaps sliding toward a loss of identity, Augustin, a loss of that person I knew long ago. Whether or not all you have said is true, the candor, spontaneity and lightheartedness that once defined you seem far from us now…

Letter VIIII
To Adeline

Adeline,

The coldness of your words surprises me! What have I said to offend you? You have saddened me to the depths of my soul. Doesn't anything of our relation remain in your heart? Today, I am much more the "Augustin" you always knew than I ever could have been at that time in our lives. Understand, my love, that my journey, from continent to continent, only reinforced the vision I already had of our respective families and the world that surrounds us. Have you ever had the desire to take a step closer to the truth? "What truth?" you would ask me. Allow me to reply even before the question settles in your mind: The only and unique truth is the one that creates this rupture with the world of the superficial, the one that allows us to move closer to reality. And not simply the reality of the world as it is or as we would like to see it, but the reality that has the obligation of opening our eyes to who we are and the projects that accompany us as persons and humanists.

Wouldn't you like to see something other than what you saw this evening? What do you truly think of the sincerity of these guests, who have done no more than fill space in the castle's ballroom? Haven't you ever dreamed of something more?

Letter X
To Augustin

Perhaps I am too young, Augustin, to understand all that you describe to me in the middle of the night? Perhaps I have unconsciously made the decision to hide from this "reality" of which you speak? Perhaps the maturity you have acquired at home, or from the paternal figures who seem to deeply influence you today, brought you to question the rules that are ever present in our society? Be honest, Augustin. Each of us plays a role, and we adapt our discourse according to those who accompany us along the way. Actor or spectator, the difference is minimal. At one moment we are the former, and the next, the latter. This allows us to peacefully exist in the society of which you have painted such a bleak picture. What touches you most at this very moment, Augustin? What is your principal preoccupation? What you are experiencing, right now, in this exchange of letters? Or what will be when our lives are merely a faded shadow in the memory of a descendent we may or may not have?

To satisfy your curiosity, I will reply. Yes. Yes, from time to time (often, to be perfectly honest), I dream of a situation that is less ambiguous. Yes, I, too, wish to touch, to feel all that is true... The suffering of one's soul, the scars of heartbreak, are the most difficult to heal, especially "when one is 17" (to cite your favorite poet). The perfect reason to protect oneself from the start.

Letter XI
To Adeline

I am happy the words of my friend Rimbaud please you! Isn't he extraordinary? So young, so passionate, so true in his writings.

Adeline, you speak of learning to protect oneself at a young age—but from what? Our family environment, wrapping us in innocence and indulgence, at the very least may be credited for offering us an idyllic picture of the world, don't you agree?

Letter XII
To Augustin

Augustin, you describe to me a happiness orchestrated by an indolent rhythm of a life constructed from passivity instead of passion! I am speaking of sentiments, my dear friend, I am speaking of the heart, of heartbreak, of sadness...

Letter XIII
To Adeline

Adeline, my sincerity and sentiments in relation to you have always been pure. You know that. To what sadness do you refer? What possibly could have happened to bring you to such words? A name! Give me a name, and I will propose a duel. This insult will not remain unpunished!

Letter XIIII
To Adeline

My dear Adeline,
 I would be surprised to imagine slumber has taken you away from me, yet my last letter remains without reply. Have I offended you? End this silence, I beg you!

Letter XV
To Adeline

Adeline,
 Your silence frightens me, leaves me in anguish. I refuse to believe you are sleeping. In any case, your maid informed my valet that you are indeed awake. Why are you waiting to reply? There is nothing you could possibly ask of me that I would not do for you! Reply, I beseech you, out of love for our youth, forever preserved in the warmth of our souls…

Letter XVI
To Augustin

Augustin,
 More than courage, it was an immeasurable effort from the most profound depths of my being that gave me the force to reply to you. You clearly have traveled the world, which opened your eyes and touched you personally. Yet you do not realize what you left behind?
 Do you have the slightest idea of what I might have felt when I learned that you left France without even telling me of your destination or hinting about the length of your absence? Why didn't you call on me one more time before your departure? Not a visit, not a word…

How could you? On the dawn of my 17th year, then, when the awareness of love and passion awakens, the hour of promises. Leaving without a word, without worrying about those who had accompanied you for so many years. Augustin, you left, casting my sentiments aside! Bewilderment: That is the pitiful conclusion your flight left in its wake… and confusion, fright. All of the emotions one can imagine were mine at one point or another. One after the next. This feeling of abandonment hurts, Augustin. It destroys. It hurts like an invisible illness that eats away at its victim, leaving wounds that will not heal. Slowly, it destroys me, yet I maintain enough breath to survive, unable to escape this torture. I would rather be a sick horse, put out of its suffering! My poor mother was an impotent spectator, day after day, as I became feverish, as I ranted and sobbed. The best doctors of Paris were called to my bedside. Poor things, they searched in vain for a rational explanation. If only they knew that a broken heart never rises intact.

I do not seek to blame you, Augustin. I do not hold you responsible for what happened to me because it was my own fault. I would have been better off casting aside the naiveté that was part of my daily life. I should have understood much earlier that I would be easy prey for the demons of love, my sentiments would fool me and I would become the ideal victim.

Letter XVII
To Adeline

Oh, my Adeline! Sweet, dear Adeline, my fragile Adeline.

How can I express what I feel as I read your letter? Never had I a clue of what was in your heart. How is it possible? How can I ever erase such injustice? How can I go on after such revelations?

Adeline, now it is you who have irrevocably torn open my heart. When I left you at that tender age, I was not seeking to turn my back on you, I was not seeking to escape. And even if after leaving you without saying a word, you felt as if your world was collapsing, please know that I had only one goal: protecting you. It is indeed that, Adeline, to protect you from a goodbye that would have lasted an eternity and caused us great heartache. I am not a coward, my gentle Adeline. I only wanted to banish unnecessary suffering, but I now realize, and unfortunately much too late, that I failed. All I hoped to avoid is exactly what unfolded before our very eyes.

Could you find the strength, in the depths of your heart, to one day forgive me? Even if it is simply a ruse meant to relieve your pain and to make me believe that this error of the past may be repaired. Do not blame yourself, Adeline, I beg you! Please understand my acts and intentions at that difficult time in my life. I could no longer breathe freely in my family's home, and I found no liberty in a future that was defined for me by past generations. As if in a coffin, closing bit by bit each day, I suffocated—to such a point that I hated myself and my own name. I wanted to come back to you as a different man, Adeline. I wanted you to rediscover me one day, almost by accident as it was at this evening's party, as someone sincere and ready for love. Love that lasts a lifetime, love that is endless and may withstand life's hardships without ever weakening. The love that I can, that I yearn to give you, Adeline, without ever asking myself a question beyond the one that preoccupies me today and for the rest of my time on this earth: What can I do to win back your love? Right at this moment, I could throw aside my pen, break the rules that oppress us and knock on your door in the middle of this cold night so that I may fall upon my knees before you! Tell me that hope still exists, tell me that I do not leave you indifferent, I implore you...

Letter XVIII
To Augustin

Augustin,

As I earlier wrote, I accuse you of nothing, and therefore nothing should weigh on you to this degree. The situation is as it is, and neither of us can rewrite the past. I want to think of the future, Augustin, and never again remind myself of that difficult moment. It seemed important and appropriate, however, to tell you of it so that all may be clear between us. At present, I would like to build a destiny of tranquility for myself. We are young, and therefore have the time to let our emotions grow and strengthen without the slightest need for haste. Do not torture yourself for what will remain unchanged, my friend. It is not worth the torment. A heart that has already known so much sadness must not suffer twice.

Letter XVIIII
To Adeline

Adeline,

I read your words without understanding them. The sweet melody of your voice resonates in my mind, but as I see your last letter, I know something is wrong. What is this barrier that you try to build between us? Why this distance? Our bodies, by nature of our situation, are denied any embrace, even as my desire to take you in my arms grows with each letter that I send, and you speak of unnecessary haste? Adeline, what has happened to you?

You, yourself, said it: Let us forget the past and live our lives today, at this very moment. But at this very moment, I only feel the coldness of dawn slipping little by little into the castle and your coldness paralyzing my body and soul! What sign are you waiting for?

Letter XX
To Augustin

Augustin,

What do you know about waiting? What do you know of the hours of agony that cut and leave you bleeding? Do not resuscitate all that I hope to escape and all that I hope never again to relive. Back in the days of the great tragedies, I would have died of heartbreak, and you would have entered the religious orders! Come out of your cocoon, Augustin, and stop inventing roles for yourself! For years, you had your chance. For years, you remained hesitant, not knowing which direction to take. For years, you played with my heart. I feel a sense of exasperation taking over, making me say I will not show you a trace of anger. I am strong, Augustin. I am no longer the little white dove, easily impressed by beautiful words.

Letter XXI
To Adeline

This is too much, Adeline! I never tarnished your honor. Certainly, you expected promises, and I left without saying goodbye. I only wanted to protect you. I was wrong, and I regret it terribly. I will regret it until the end. I unveil to you now my most sincere feelings. To push me away in that manner is wrong, Adeline. I dare to think that perhaps behind your words, as hard as the walls of this castle, exists a spark, so small, yet only asking to be reignited.

Letter XXII
To Augustin

Augustin,

Our story can no longer exist. At least not at present. You must leave me, Augustin, and turn to uncharted horizons. It would be utopic to think of building a new future this way, in the middle of the night, even as day is almost upon us...

Letter XXIII
To Adeline

Never! Do you understand, Adeline? NEVER! I refuse to let errors of the past soil our dream. I will not abandon it! If I must follow you to the ends of the earth and beg for your forgiveness, become your shadow so as never to leave you for an instant. I will make any sacrifice.

Letter XXIIII
To Augustin

Augustin,

Your passion, your words reassure me. I am not naïve. I can see love when it exists. But now it is my turn to protect you as I realize it is my responsibility to calm your ardor and tell you to hold onto your promises. The idea of losing you again is unbearable, and in spite of my late declaration of affection for you, reality enchains us, Augustin. I must go. I leave at sunrise. I will be joining my great-aunt in Austria.

Letter XXV
To Adeline

I will follow you. I will meet you there in less than two days, just the time to free myself from my obligations here, and I will be at your side.

Letter XXVI
To Augustin

No, Augustin, this time apart will be good—for you and for me. I decided to spend a year in Vienna and continue my studies of music there. And I will not hide the second reason for this trip: I would not miss *Carmen* for anything in the world. The performances began several weeks ago at the Vienna opera house. Bizet no longer lives, as you know, but his masterpiece has triumphed. From Wagner to Brahms, all are under his charm. I even heard that the latter attended more than 20 shows! I want to experience this joy that awaits me, and then I want to be alone, to focus on my cello and my studies. A year, Augustin. Four little seasons. Could we possibly hope to reunite? Would you have the courage to wait for me? Am I being reasonable, asking you such a thing? Will the purity of our sentiments withstand this test?

Letter XXVII
To Adeline

I am yours, body and soul, Adeline, and I understand your motivations. Keep me in your heart, and upon your return, let us promise to breathe the same air, to share the same warmth, to live each day as if tomorrow might never exist, as if every morning would give us a new chance to fall in love with each other once again, over and over. Day after day, you will hear from me in Vienna, Adeline: In the evening, alone at my desk, my pen will fill pages with words of a passion that will only grow, without ever faltering.

Letter XXVIII
To Augustin

Shall we make a promise at this very moment, Augustin, to return here to this castle in a year, to this very spot? As if time had stopped. Will we then continue this nighttime correspondence before falling into each other's arms for eternity?

Letter XXVIIII
To Adeline

Adeline,

Your words are music to my ears, and I am eager to write the 365th letter before, finally, holding you in my arms.

Night is coming to an end, Adeline, and I know that your great-aunt is expecting you. I will write a final letter at daybreak, and I will hide it in the secret compartment of the desk in your room after your departure. You will find it when you return in a year, in memory of this marvelous and unforgettable night.

Letter XXX
To Augustin

I will not say "goodbye," my love. I will leave you with a simple "until we meet again." And now I must go.

Your Adeline, always and forever.

Letter XXXI
To Adeline

My dear Adeline,

This night marks the unfolding of a story of all ages. The flame of my candle is weak, the ink in my pen is dry. The fog of dawn rolling through the castle's grounds does not hide your silhouette in front of the carriage awaiting you below. From the window of my room, my eyes envelop you in a protective shroud that will accompany you during 12 long months as I wait for our reunion. My heart is heavy as I watch you depart, but at the same time, in ecstasy at the idea that you are closer to being mine with each passing day, each passing hour.

When you hold this letter, we will be about to meet once again. I imagine you, breathing rapidly, hands trembling, overcome with emotion as my footsteps approach your door. I will knock three times, you will rush forth, and together we will fall into each other's arms, locked for eternity.

Your Augustin, forever and always.

NOTE

On the following pages, we present to you "Letters of the Night" in its original French version.

Les lettres de la nuit
(Adeline et Augustin)
Didier Quémener

Les faits racontés se présentent comme pure fiction. Seuls les personnages de cette correspondance pourraient témoigner de la véracité du récit. Adeline et Augustin racontent l'amour. D'une histoire de jeunesse, alors tous deux enfants se jouant des règles qu'une vie d'adulte leur imposerait, naîtra un véritable attachement réciproque. Leur récente rencontre, au Château de Madame de M. pendant l'hiver 1875, sera le moment opportun de raviver une passion dépassant l'imagination du commun des lecteurs. Les lettres reproduites dans cette histoire vous sont livrées telles qu'elles furent retrouvées, sans avoir été éditées et sans aucune modification de leur contenu.

Lettre I
A Adeline

Chère Adeline,
Pardonnez mon arrogance alors que je vous fais

parvenir cette missive à une heure si tardive de la nuit mais il m'était impossible de trouver le sommeil, tant votre présence ce soir pendant la réception donnée au Château a occulté le reste de la fête et de ses invités.

Mon esprit s'est dérobé à la minute où mon regard s'est posé sur votre visage. Certes je retrouve, en admirant la jeune-femme que vous êtes devenue, l'enfant que je connaissais lors de mes visites ponctuelles au domaine familial. Cependant le temps semble me narguer alors que je vois encore dans vos yeux nos jeux d'été d'hier, dans le parc derrière la demeure parentale, et que je devine aujourd'hui toute l'élégance et la grâce qui vous ont accompagnée au cours de cette cérémonie. Ces quelques années, sans jamais vous revoir une fois, ont laissé sur vous une empreinte si délicate, si légère... Si Madame de M. n'avait pas fait les présentations, je serais certainement resté encore de nombreuses années sans jamais vous apercevoir de nouveau. Quel plaisir d'avoir pu vous voir encore ! Si l'assoupissement et la fatigue ne vous ont pas encore gagnée, une réponse de votre part conclurait ces belles retrouvailles.

Lettre II
A Augustin

Cher Augustin,

Vous êtes tout pardonné puisque je ne dormais pas. A vrai dire, en cherchant dans mes souvenirs et me remémorant le jeune adolescent fougueux que vous étiez, je n'en attendais pas moins de vous. Un silence de votre part m'aurait certainement surprise. Le plaisir est réciproque Augustin. Ces années passées à l'étranger vous ont muri, semble-t-il ? Vous apparaissez en homme du monde instruit et votre comportement, plein d'assurance dans vos conversations avec vos compères, vous donne belle allure en société, surtout devant la gente féminine comme j'ai pu le remarquer... Félicitations !

Lettre III
A Adeline

Adeline,

Je vous remercie pour vos mots. Vous avez raison : ces voyages m'ont beaucoup apporté, tant intellectuellement qu'humainement. Et puis le temps qui s'écoule inexorablement marque son empreinte sur vous, comme cette encre sur les lettres que je vous adresse. Saviez-vous que j'ai précieusement gardé les quelques lettres que vous m'écriviez lors de vos hivers en Italie avec vos parents ? Quand la mélancolie vient frapper aux portes de mon cœur, je les relis, l'une après l'autre... Avez-vous encore les miennes ?

Lettre IIII
A Augustin

Je crois que vos lettres sont toujours à la résidence hivernale que nous occupions mais après la prise de Rome, mes parents se sont installés à Florence depuis peu. Il se peut qu'elles y soient déjà arrivées : l'ancienne Capitale est devenue si politiquement instable que mon père a décidé de se séparer de notre maison de famille. C'est bien triste, je vous l'avoue Augustin. J'ai le sentiment qu'une partie de moi va s'éteindre le jour où j'apprendrai la vente. Mais il en est ainsi, comme pour ce qui est de la vie. Les choses changent et nous changeons avec elles.

Lettre V
A Adeline

La vie ne vaut d'être vécue, Adeline, que si l'on craint de la perdre : si l'irremplaçable disparaît, à quoi bon continuer une existence dépourvue de son principal intérêt ? La simple idée de perdre la moindre chose qui me rattache à vous me glacerait le sang. Je n'ose y songer ! J'achèterai la maison romaine de vos parents et contacterai mon ami l'Ambassadeur de France afin qu'il prenne toutes les mesures nécessaires pour en assurer sa sécurité. Le temps nous appartient pour que nous y laissions notre trace, pour que nos souvenirs s'enracinent à jamais.

Lettre VI
A Augustin

Augustin, voici qui est bien noble de votre part et tout à votre honneur : je vous en remercie. Je ferai part de vos intentions à mon père qui ne manquera pas de vous contacter à ce sujet. Mais dites-moi, votre réussite sociale est remarquable : nous n'avons pas eu l'occasion de beaucoup converser lors de cette soirée, quel est donc votre milieu professionnel ? Avez-vous suivi les affaires de feu votre grand-père ? Le commerce des métaux précieux semble plus que jamais prolifique.

Lettre VII
A Adeline

Les affaires sont les affaires. Les relations avec mon père, que vous avez bien connu, se sont lentement dégradées provoquant mon départ de voyage autour du monde. Il a toujours refusé de comprendre mon désir de liberté, ce qui me fait penser parfois que l'exemple de sa vie m'a servi de point de repère d'une certaine manière. Je voulais à tout prix m'éloigner de l'enfermement financier dans lequel il se trouvait happé un peu plus chaque jour. Voilà pourquoi j'ai eu très tôt le désir de partir : quitter cet esclavage cupide, quitter ce mal incessant qui le rongeait comme une maladie invisible. Je me suis construit seul Adeline, seul au fur et à mesure de mes rencontres. Cette expérience, éloignée de la vie mondaine que vous et moi avions connue depuis notre plus jeune âge, a de loin été la meilleure de ces dernières années. J'ai vu des gens qui ne possédaient rien et dont l'unique richesse se résumait à leur quotidien : manger pour survivre. J'ai côtoyé des familles dont les enfants se mettaient à travailler à partir du moment où ils avaient assez de force pour tenir sur leurs deux jambes. J'ai vu la misère Adeline, la pauvreté dans son pire état. J'ai vu la tristesse de visages fermés sur lesquels le temps semble soudain s'arrêter pour creuser, jour après jour, un peu plus de souffrance.

Ne vous fiez pas aux apparences des futilités d'il y a quelques heures : tout ceci n'est qu'un jeu de dupes. Je n'éprouve aucune honte à me servir d'eux, aucun remords pour faire semblant d'appartenir à leur monde, aucun regret de les utiliser à mon gré. La vérité Adeline c'est que votre souvenir d'un Augustin que vous connaissiez jusqu'alors ne devra rester qu'un souvenir parmi tant d'autres. Je suis libre de mes actes et je décide de mon destin, au contraire de mon père. D'avoir atteint l'âge adulte aura au moins eu ce mérite de me proclamer affranchi. Et cette indépendance n'a pas de prix.

Lettre VIII
A Augustin

Mon cher Augustin,

Votre histoire est aussi singulière qu'émouvante. Qui aurait imaginé un tel sort et de telles aventures ? Je suis loin d'imaginer que vous regrettiez tout de même le milieu qui vous a façonné ? Que gardez-vous de nos sentiments d'enfants ? Une douce amertume qui d'un côté vous rattache à moi et de l'autre vous en éloigne fatalement, à en juger votre dédain pour cette classe sociale qui nous a vus naître ? Vouloir renoncer à une partie de son passé ou bien encore croire à l'abandon de ses origines sont bien plus profonds, à mon sens, qu'un état de faits (aussi fondamental qu'il puisse être) : vous glissez peut-être également vers une perte d'identité Augustin, une perte de l'être que j'ai connu auparavant. Fausse ou vraie hypocrisie, la candeur, la juvénilité et la spontanéité qui vous définissaient me paraissent si loin…

Lettre VIIII
A Adeline

Adeline,

Votre froideur à mon égard me surprend ! Que dis-je ? M'effraie et m'attriste au plus profond de mon âme ! Ne reste-t-il rien de notre relation dans votre cœur ? Je suis aujourd'hui bien plus l'« Augustin » que vous avez toujours connu que je n'ai pu l'être à cette époque de nos vies. Au contraire, comprenez ma chère et tendre que mon périple, de continent en continent, n'a fait que renforcer la vision déjà altérée que j'avais du monde qui nous entourait, vous et moi, dans nos familles respectives. N'avez-vous jamais eu le désir de vous rapprocher de la vérité ? Quelle vérité me direz-vous ?

Permettez-moi de vous répondre avant même que la question ne vous traverse l'esprit : la seule et unique vérité, celle qui crée cette rupture avec le monde des faux-semblants qui nous inonde, celle qui nous permet de nous rapprocher imperceptiblement de la réalité. Et pas seulement une réalité du monde tel qu'il est ou tel que nous devrions tous le voir, mais la réalité, cette réalité qui a pour obligation de nous ouvrir les yeux sur ce que nous sommes et du dessein qui nous accompagne en tant que personne, en tant qu'humaniste.

N'aimeriez-vous pas voir autre chose que ce dont vous avez été témoin ce soir ? Que pensez-vous réellement de la sincérité des gens qui ne faisaient que finalement emplir l'espace décadent du Château ? N'avez-vous enfin jamais rêvé à autre chose ?

Lettre X
A Augustin

Peut-être étais-je trop jeune Augustin pour voir tout ce que vous me décrivez au beau milieu de la nuit ? Peut-être avais-je pris inconsciemment la décision de cacher cette « réalité » dont vous parlez ? Peut-être votre maturité acquise au sein de votre famille, ou devrais-je dire devant ces figures paternelles qui semblent encore vous hanter aujourd'hui, a su vous apporter cette pensée indécise sur les règles qui sont malgré tout présentes autour de nous ? Soyons honnêtes Augustin : nous jouons tous un rôle et nous adaptons notre discours en fonction de celles et ceux qui nous accompagnent dans notre chemin. Acteur ou spectateur, la différence est infime, Nous basculons tantôt d'un côté, tantôt de l'autre. C'est ce qui nous autorise à évoluer « sereinement » dans cette société dont vous peignez un tableau bien sombre. Que vous importe le plus à ce moment précis Augustin ? Quelle est votre première préoccupation ? Ce que vous vivez là, en cet instant, dans l'échange de nos lettres, ou bien ce qu'il adviendra quand notre existence ne sera plus qu'une légère trace dans la mémoire d'une quelconque descendance que nous n'aurons peut-être pas ?

Pour satisfaire votre curiosité, je vous répondrai oui. Oui j'ai parfois (souvent pour être parfaitement honnête) rêvé d'une situation moins ambigüe. Oui j'ai pareillement eu envie de sentir, toucher ou ne serait-ce qu'effleurer le vrai, du bout des doigts. Les peines de l'âme, les cicatrices du cœur sont celles dont on guéri le plus difficilement, surtout « quand on a dix-sept ans » (pour reprendre l'âge fétiche de votre poète préféré) : raison s'il en fallait une pour apprendre à se protéger dès les prémices de l'adolescence.

Lettre XI
A Adeline

Je suis heureux de voir que mon ami Rimbaud vous plaise ! N'est-il pas extraordinaire ? Si jeune, si ardent, si juste dans son écriture !

Adeline, vous dites avoir appris, dès votre plus jeune âge, à vous protéger : mais de quoi ? L'innocence du cocon familial qui nous a choyés tous les deux durant tant d'années aura au moins eu le mérite de nous faire croire à un monde idyllique et de nous faire vivre une insouciance non négligeable, ne pensez-vous pas ?

Lettre XII
A Augustin

Augustin, vous me décrivez un bonheur orchestré au rythme indolent d'une vie construite dans une oisiveté bien plus affligeante que passionnante ! Je vous parle de sentiments mon cher ami, je vous parle du cœur, de peine, de tristesse…

Lettre XIII
A Adeline

Adeline, ma sincérité et mes sentiments envers vous ont toujours été purs, vous le savez. A quelles douleurs faites-vous allusions ? Qu'a bien-t-il pu vous arriver pour tenir de tels propos ? Un nom ! Donnez-moi un nom et je m'efforcerai de braver ce briseur d'amour et panserai vos blessures : un tel affront ne restera pas impuni !

Lettre XIIII
A Adeline

Ma chère Adeline,
Je serai surpris de vous savoir assoupie et pourtant ma dernière lettre est restée sans réponse : vous ai-je offensée en quoi que ce soit ? Répondez-moi, je vous en conjure !

Lettre XV
A Adeline

Adeline,

Votre mutisme m'épouvante, m'angoisse. Je me refuse à croire que vous dormiez. Et d'ailleurs mon valet de chambre m'a fait savoir par votre servante que vous étiez toujours éveillée. Qu'attendez-vous pour me répondre ? Inutile de vous répéter qu'il n'existe rien au monde que vous ne puissiez me demander et que je me refuse à faire pour vous ! Répondez-moi, par amour de notre jeunesse préservée dans la chaleur de nos âmes !

Lettre XVI
A Augustin

Augustin,

Bien plus que du courage, c'est un effort incommensurable qu'il m'a fallu pour trouver, au plus confiné de mon être, la force de vous répondre. Vous avez évidemment parcouru le monde, ce qui vous a ouvert les yeux et interpellé personnellement, sans pour autant vous rendre compte de ce que vous laissiez derrière vous ?

Avez-vous la moindre idée de ce que j'ai pu ressentir lorsque j'ai appris que vous quittiez la France sans même m'avertir sur votre destination ni la sur durée de votre voyage ? Pourquoi n'êtes-vous pas venu me rendre visite une dernière fois avant votre départ ? Pas une visite, pas un mot : comment avez-vous pu ? A l'aube de mes dix-sept printemps, à l'heure de l'éveil à l'amour et aux passions, à l'heure des promesses ! Partir sans mot dire, partir sans vous soucier de celles et ceux qui vous ont accompagné durant tant d'année ? Enfin Augustin, partir en laissant mes sentiments aux abois ! Désemparée : voilà la triste conclusion que votre envol a pu laisser comme traces dans ma vie de jeune femme… Le désarroi, la peur : je suis passée par tous les sentiments, l'un succédant à l'autre ! Prenez le temps de la réflexion Augustin car je vous laisse imaginer tous les synonymes que la langue française possède. Cette sensation d'abandon vous fait mal Augustin. Elle détruit. Elle fait mal comme une maladie invisible qui vous ronge et ne guérit pas, qui vous tue lentement et vous garde assez de souffle pour en souffrir sans jamais pour autant vous achever. J'aurais préféré être un cheval malade que l'on se doit d'abattre afin ne plus le voir râler de douleur ! Ma pauvre mère a été spectatrice impuissante, jour après jour, de mes poussées de fièvres, de mes lamentations, de mes sanglots. Les médecins du tout Paris se sont succédé à mon chevet : les pauvres, ils cherchaient en vain une explication rationnelle à mes maux… Si seulement ils savaient qu'un cœur brisé, mis à terre, ne se relève jamais intact ?

Je ne cherche pas à vous blâmer Augustin, je ne vous tiens pas pour responsable de ce qui m'est arrivé car tout est de ma propre faute. J'aurais dû oublier cette naïveté qui faisait mon quotidien, j'aurais dû comprendre beaucoup plus tôt que je serais une proie facile face aux démons de l'amour, que mes sentiments se joueraient de moi et que je deviendrais finalement la victime idéale.

Lettre XVII
A Adeline

Oh Adeline ! Chère et tendre Adeline, ma douce, fragile Adeline…

Une fois n'est pas coutume, les mots me manquent pour exprimer ce que je ressens à la lecture de votre lettre… Je n'ai jamais appris de quiconque ce dont vous venez de me faire part ! Comment est-ce possible ? Comment puis-je un jour effacer une telle injustice ? Comment vais-je être capable de supporter mon être après de telles révélations ?

Adeline, vous venez d'ouvrir mon cœur à vif et je crains, à mon tour, qu'il ne se referme jamais... Lorsque je vous ai laissée à la fin de votre adolescence, je ne cherchais pas à vous fuir, je n'étais pas en exil. Même si, en vous quittant sans mot dire, vous avez cru voir votre monde s'écrouler, je l'ai fait dans un but unique : vous épargner. C'est bien cela Adeline, vous éviter toute douleur inutile d'un au revoir qui aurait semblé une éternité et qui nous aurait certainement meurtris l'un et l'autre. Je ne suis pas un lâche ma belle Adeline, j'ai voulu uniquement nous empêcher des souffrances superflues mais je constate, malheureusement bien trop tard, que j'ai échoué et que c'est tout le contraire de ma pensée qui s'est réalisé devant vos yeux.

Trouverez-vous la force, au plus profond de votre cœur, pour me pardonner un jour ? Ne serait-ce que dans l'illusion d'alléger votre peine et me faire croire ainsi que cette erreur d'un passé pas si lointain est réparable ? Ne vous accablez pas Adeline, je vous en supplie ! Comprenez mon geste et mes intentions à cette époque désagréable de ma vie : je ne pouvais plus respirer au sein de ma propre famille, je ne voyais aucune liberté dans un avenir qui m'était alors tout tracé par héritage de mes aïeuls. Comme un cercueil se refermant un peu plus chaque jour sur moi, je suffoquais jusqu'à en haïr mon propre nom et ma naissance. Je voulais vous revenir autrement Adeline, je voulais que vous me redécouvriez un jour, par le gré du hasard comme ce fut (presque) le cas ce soir, en tant qu'homme sincère et en définitive prêt pour l'amour. L'amour d'une vie entière, l'amour qui brûle incommensurablement et qui traverse les épreuves de la vie dans jamais s'éteindre ou même s'affaiblir.

L'amour que je peux, que je veux vous donner Adeline, sans réfléchir, sans regarder autour de nous, sans ne plus me poser aucune autre question que celle qui me préoccupe aujourd'hui pour le reste de mon parcours sur cette terre : que dois-je faire pour regagner votre amour en retour ? Je peux sur le champ lâcher cette plume, briser toutes les lois dérisoires qui nous oppressent et venir frapper à votre porte au milieu de cette nuit glaciale pour tomber à genoux devant vous ! Dites-moi que l'espoir existe encore, dites-moi que je ne vous laisse pas indifférente, je vous en supplie !

Lettre XVIII
A Augustin

Augustin,

Comme je vous l'ai écrit, je ne vous accuse de rien et de ce fait, rien non plus ne doit vous accabler à ce point. Les choses sont ce qu'elles ont été et ni vous ni moi ne referons le passé. Je veux penser à l'avenir Augustin et ne plus me remémorer cette parenthèse, aussi pénible soit-elle, de ma jeune vie. Il m'a semblé important et approprié de vous le raconter pour que tout soit clair entre nous. A présent, je veux me construire une destinée paisible. Nous sommes jeunes, ce qui laisse le temps à nos émois de grandir et de s'affirmer sans la moindre précipitation. Ne vous torturez pas pour ce qui restera inchangé mon ami, cela n'en vaut pas le tourment : tout le malheur d'un cœur, qui a déjà connu tant de souffrances, ne doit jamais se répéter.

Lettre XVIIII
A Adeline

Adeline,

Je vous lis sans pour autant vous comprendre. La mélodie de votre voix douce résonne dans ma tête lorsque je lis vos mots mais ce que mes yeux voient sonne faux. Quel est donc cet écart que vous essayez sans interruption d'imposer entre nos êtres ? Pourquoi cette distance ? Nos corps sont, par la force des choses, éloignés de toute étreinte alors que mon désir de vous prendre dans mes bras s'enflamme toujours un peu plus après chaque lettre que je vous envoie et vous me parlez de temps en suspens, de précipitation inutile ? Adeline, que vous arrive-t-il ? Vous venez vous-même de l'exprimer : oublions le passé et vivons notre vie aujourd'hui, à ce moment précis. Mais en cet instant, je ne ressens que la froidure de l'aube qui envahit peu à peu le Château et la vôtre qui me transperce de toute part, me paralyse le corps et m'ankylose l'âme ! A quelle étoile funèbre vous fiez-vous ? Qu'attendez-vous du ciel ?

Lettre XX
A Augustin

Augustin,

Que savez-vous de l'attente ? Que connaissez-vous des heures d'agonie qui vous entaillent et vous laissent à vif ? Ne faites pas ressusciter ce que je m'attache à enfouir et ne veux plus jamais vivre une nouvelle fois. Au temps des grandes tragédies anciennes, je serais morte de chagrin et vous seriez entré dans les ordres ! Sortez de votre coquille de soie Augustin et cessez de vous inventer des rôles sur mesure ! Pendant des années vous avez eu votre chance, pendant des années vous n'avez cessé d'être hésitant, se sachant pas quelle direction prendre, pendant des années vous avez joué avec mes sentiments… Mais je sens l'exaspération qui me gagne ce qui me fait dire que je ne veux vous montrer aucune colère, aucune contrition. Je suis forte Augustin, je ne suis plus cette petite oie blanche, appât facile, de mots et de belles paroles.

Lettre XXI
A Adeline

Cela en est trop Adeline ! Je ne vous ai ni bafouée, ni sali votre honneur de quelconque façon qu'il puisse être ! Vous attendiez des promesses, certes, et je suis parti sans vous revoir. Je cherchais à vous protéger : j'ai eu tort et je le regrette infiniment. Je le regretterai jusque la fin de mes jours. En ce lieu, je vous dévoile mes émotions les plus sincères. Me repousser de la sorte est un mensonge Adeline. Je n'ose croire que derrière vos mots, aussi durs que la pierre des murs de cette demeure, si brutaux et violents, il n'existe pas une flamme, si infime soit-elle, ne demandant qu'à être ravivée.

Lettre XXII
A Augustin

Augustin,
Notre histoire ne peut plus exister. En tout cas pas maintenant. Vous devez me laisser Augustin, vous devez vous tourner vers de nouveaux horizons. Ce serait utopique que de penser à construire un avenir, ainsi en pleine nuit, alors que le jour ne va pas tarder à se lever…

Lettre XXIII
A Adeline

Jamais ! Comprenez-vous Adeline, JAMAIS ! Je ne laisserai pas les erreurs du passé souiller notre rêve, je n'abandonnerai pas ! Si je devais vous suivre jusqu'au bout du monde et implorer votre pardon, devenir votre ombre pour ne plus jamais vous quitter un seul instant, je ferais tous les sacrifices pour y parvenir.

Lettre XXIIII
A Augustin

Augustin,

Votre élan, votre passion, vos mots me rassurent. Je ne suis pas naïve. Je vois l'amour. Mais c'est à mon tour de vous protéger car je sens bien qu'il en va de ma responsabilité de freiner vos ardeurs en vous disant de garder vos promesses. La pensée de vous perdre encore m'est insupportable et malgré un aveu tardif de mon affection pour vous, la réalité de notre quotidien nous enchaîne Augustin. Il vous faut renoncer mon bel amant. Je dois vous quitter. Je pars dès le lever du soleil retrouver ma grand-tante en Autriche.

Lettre XXV
A Adeline

Je vous suis ! Je vous rejoins sur place dans moins de deux jours, le temps de parer aux obligations qui me tiennent et je serai à vos côtés.

Lettre XXVI
A Augustin

Non Augustin, l'isolement sera bienfaiteur : aussi
bien pour vous que pour moi. J'ai décidé de rester un an
à Vienne et parfaire mon apprentissage de la musique. De
plus, et je ne cache pas mon égoïsme, je ne manquerais
pour rien au monde Carmen dont les représentations
viennent de débuter il y a seulement quelques semaines à
l'Opéra impérial. Bizet n'est plus, comme vous le savez
hélas, mais son chef-d'œuvre a reçu un véritable
triomphe ces derniers jours. De Wagner a Brahms, tous
sont tombés sous le charme ! J'ai même entendu dire que
ce dernier aurait déjà assisté à plus d'une vingtaine de
représentations, vous rendez-vous compte ? Je veux vivre
cette extase qui m'attend dans moins de deux jours et
ensuite m'isoler, me recueillir avec mon violoncelle et
mon travail. Une année Augustin, quatre petites saisons :
pouvons-nous espérer nous retrouver ? Aurez-vous
l'audace de m'attendre ? Suis-je raisonnable de vous
demander un tel dévouement ? La pureté de nos
sentiments résistera-t-elle à cette épreuve ?

Lettre XXVII
A Adeline

Je vous suis corps et âme Adeline ! Qui d'autre que
moi comprendrait le mieux vos motivations ? Gardez-
moi dans votre cœur et dès votre retour, promettons-
nous de respirer le même air, de partager la même
chaleur, de vivre chaque jour comme s'il n'y avait aucun
lendemain à considérer, comme si nos vies étaient à bout
de souffle et que chaque matin nous donne une nouvelle
chance de nous séduire, de nous conquérir encore et
toujours… Jour après jour, vous recevrez de mes

nouvelles à Vienne Adeline : le soir venu, seul devant mon bureau, ma plume comblera des pages blanches où vous lirez ma passion qui ne fera que grandir sans jamais flétrir.

Lettre XXVIII
A Augustin

Prenons date en cet instant précis Augustin et retrouvons-nous, dans un an au Château de Madame de M., en cet endroit même : nous échangerons alors peut-être nos ultimes lettres avant de nous retrouver dans les bras l'un de l'autre et nous enlacer pour l'éternité ?

Lettre XXVIIII
A Adeline

Adeline,

Vos désirs sont mélodie à mes oreilles et il me tarde d'achever la trois-cent-soixante-cinquième lettre avant de pouvoir enfin vous serrer, vous embrasser.

La nuit touche à sa fin Adeline et je sais que vous êtes attendue. Je rédigerai une dernière lettre, pour cette nuit, que je dissimulerai dans le compartiment secret du bureau de votre chambre après votre départ. Vous la trouverez à votre retour, dans un an, en mémoire de cette nuit merveilleuse et ineffaçable.

Lettre XXX
A Augustin

Je ne vous dis pas « au revoir » mon bel amant : je vous laisse avec simple « à tout à l'heure » en guise d'adieu. Je pars.

Votre Adeline, pour toujours et à jamais.

Lettre XXXI
A Adeline

Ma belle Adeline,

La flamme de ma bougie se fait si frêle, l'encre de ma plume se fait si rare… Cette nuit a marqué d'un sceau immuable une histoire qui appartient à l'éternité des âges. Le brouillard de l'aube qui envahit l'esplanade du Château ne peut dissimuler votre silhouette devant la voiture vous attendant plus bas. De la fenêtre ma chambre, mes yeux vous enveloppent d'un linceul protecteur qui vous accompagnera pendant ces douze longs mois où je resterai à vous attendre. Mon cœur est lourd en observant votre départ mais également si bouillonnant à l'idée que vous serez mienne, toujours un peu plus, d'heures en heures, de jours en jours.

Lorsque vous tiendrez cette lettre entre vos mains, nous serons à quelques mètres l'un de l'autre. Je vous imaginerai respiration haletante, mains tremblantes, submergée d'émoi, alors que mes pas résonneront dans le couloir qui mène à votre chambre. Je frapperai trois fois sur votre porte, vous vous précipiterez pour m'ouvrir et nous tomberont ensemble sur le sol, étreints pour l'éternité.

Votre Augustin, à jamais et pour toujours.

Sonny's Wall
Paula Young Lee

Across the street, Sonny's building a wall. He's not building it for himself. He's building the wall for my neighbor on the kitchen side of the house. I doubt he's getting paid for the work. I think he's doing it for the privilege of leaving his mark on the world, one gravestone at a time.

At 80, Sonny's grizzled and tattooed, with tufted thin hair that sticks out from both sides of his head. He's podgy in the belly, carrying all his weight in front like a lot of old men do. He's lost most of his hair to old age, one kidney to infection, his gallbladder to gallstones, his thyroid to cancer, and his colon to irritability. Thanks to a pair of unusually strong forearms and a permanent forward stoop, he looks like Old Popeye and talks like him too, with lots of yarls, murls and other unintelligible burrs. After he got out of the Army, he went to work as a gravedigger. The stones he's using came from the cemetery where he used to work.

A half-century of manual labor has created calluses so

thick Sonny doesn't need gloves. With arthritic fingers so stubby they look as if they've lost their tips, he tests each stone for qualities I cannot discern. He lifts each one—a small boulder, really—hugging it close to his body as he carries the stone pregnancy hunched over and bowlegged, walking it the few yards to the spot where it goes. Carefully, he fits the stones together with such precision that the thinnest slick of mortar helps them stick together. Gravity does the real work.

Every day, rain or shine, what's left of him goes out and adds ancient stones to the retaining wall keeping four feet of rising dirt from turning into mud and sliding into the road. Does it matter that he's building the wall for a jerk? The Jerk's house sits in the middle of a quarter-acre of land seeded with beer cans. Every night, The Jerk's brood sits on the picturesque porch, smoking whatever's handy. Drunk, the boys like to flick cigarette butts at our house, hoping to accidentally start a fire.

The wall doesn't care. Neither does Sonny. Stone by stone, hour after day after month after year, the wall rises. He is in no hurry. This wall cannot be rushed. He is building it to stand long after there is no one to take care of it.

As Sonny's wall rises, Maggie's house falls.

Sonny's wall is an L shape, buttressing an irregular plot that rises into a hill, then flattens out on the back side of the house. My house faces the long arm of the L. Her house faces the short arm.

Masking tape holds the windows of her house together. Hanging off their hinges, the shutters swing in the breeze. The roof is going bald. The siding is peeling off in great sheets, airing out the rotting wood slats underneath. It's like seeing a face with its skin removed, exposing a precarious armature of tendons and bones.

The entire caboodle seems ready to collapse at any moment.

Maggie's a demented old lady with a miniature terrier. Obese and ill-tempered, Skipper greets the day by evacuating his bowels in my backyard. Thanks to the odd physical configuration of my neighborhood on the pond, the back windows of my dining room are eye level with his butt, giving me a daily eyeful of the doggie squat from underneath and close up. I tried shooing him away, but Maggie just leans over and peers through the window, making me feel like a fish in a bowl as her mouth moves in silent mutters. I've gotten used to seeing Maggie's pale wrinkled face pressed up against my windowpanes, angling for a better look at the strange sight of two people breakfasting while naked.

Abruptly, John's head pops out from behind *The Wall Street Journal.*

"Do you hear that?" he demands. "Somebody's stuck."

"Yah, I heard it." I nod, just in time to catch a glimpse of Maggie's ghostly face vanishing from the window. I just figured it was Sonny. Yesterday he was hauling off debris.

Grumbling, John rises from the table, wraps a towel around his waist and thuds onto the porch. A few minutes later, he comes thudding back into the house with his lips drawn down in a deep scowl.

"Go look," he says dourly. "A really big one is out there."

Every winter, delivery trucks end up stuck in the road running between my kitchen and Sonny's wall. But yesterday it was 80 degrees. There's no ice on the ground and no snow narrowing the roads. Yet there it is: a full-sized furniture delivery truck. Thoroughly stuck.

Screeeeeee! the spinning wheels complain.

Pulling on my bathrobe, I stick my face out the door

to the front porch and declare to nobody in particular: "There's no way they're getting out of there without a tow."

John looks out the windows and scowls again.

"Hey!" he yells loudly, and storms outside in a towel before I can stop him. "Stop taking apart the wall!"

The truck drivers have tried pulling. They've tried pushing. And now, they've taken logs from our woodpile and rocks from Sonny's wall. The plan seems to be an attempt to build a teeter-totter out of the pilfered materials. By the back tires, they've erected a sort of cairn using Sonny's stones. By leaning our firewood on the makeshift fulcrum, they've created a lopsided ramp.

I can hear the drivers halfheartedly apologizing for stealing our materials, but mostly they're thinking that John's an asshole. John storms back inside and calls the cops.

CRUNCH!

Splintered wood is scattered in the street, but the big truck is now forward a few feet and no longer stuck. It trundles away, leaving a great pile of smashed wood and broken stones in the middle of the road. It looks like the corpse of a homicide victim.

A group of neighborhood women are standing outside Maggie's house, milling by Sonny's pile of stones. I go outside to find out what's going on.

"Maggie died last night," my neighbor June says directly. "Do you want Skipper?"

"No thanks!" I reply, flustered. "I, uh, I don't like tiny dogs!"

June sighs. "Her sisters are trying to get me to take it. But I can't."

"Someone will take it," I lie. No one will take Skipper, because he's a horrible, horrible dog. "Do you know if the sisters have plans for lunch?"

"I don't know," June says hesitantly.

I head over to Maggie's front door and poke my head in.

"Hello?" I call out.

There's no answer, but the remnants of the screen door are propped open. The regular door is swinging loosely, barely clinging to the jamb as it dangles from badly rusted hinges. Gingerly, I push the door all the way open and find myself staring at a kitchen that looks as if it hasn't been cleaned for several decades. Grime coats every surface. The linoleum is peeling up in great, dirt-encrusted chunks. The interior is stuffed full of garbage.

And yet there are signs of the woman she used to be: a china cabinet lined with porcelain teacups, a collection of curio cats, embroidered tea towels, piles of hardcover books. Most touchingly, there are crude watercolors scattered atop great piles of junk. They are paintings of the swans on our pond. Maggie's living room window is clouded, broken and patched with sad strips of masking tape, but I can see the swans through them, swimming whitely on the water sparkling in the late summer sun.

"Hello?" I call out again. "Anyone home?"

"Hullo?" A small cream-colored woman bustles into the kitchen to greet me. She is British in accent and demeanor, a slight smile playing around the corners of her mouth, topped by apple cheeks. She has the British trick of wringing her hands ever so slightly and phrasing every statement as a question. "I'm Elaine?" she says helpfully.

"June told me you're Maggie's sister," I say.

Elaine nods.

"I'm one of the neighbors. The brown house with all the stuff on the porch." I point in the general direction of my house. "I've made noodles and a pie. Would you like to join us?"

"Oh, thank you," she replies politely. "But we're going to Pam's for lunch, then we're coming back to do more with the house." She clearly thinks I know who Pam is, but I don't have a clue.

"You're not trying to… clean?" I ask uncertainly. Maggie was a hoarder in full depths of her illness. Ages ago, for one reason or another, she began using jars instead of plumbing. It smells in here.

"Goodness, no!" she replies. "The junk man is coming on Thursday to take everything out. Then the house will be razed." As she chats, another woman comes down the stairs. Much younger than her sister, she is wearing rubber utility gloves and has the air of someone used to tackling big jobs with good cheer.

"I'm Linda," she says in friendly tones. Maggie's other sister. She waves instead of extending her hand on account of the rubber gloves.

"Did you come from England for the funeral?"

They both nod. "I never visited her before," Elaine says wistfully. "Now I wish I had. Everyone is so lovely."

"Oh yes," I lie. "We're all just wonderful!"

I learn that Elaine and her sister both live in England, and they share the same father as Maggie but not the same mother. They hardly knew each other because they were barely born by the time Maggie left home.

This explains the sisters' marked lack of bereavement. Some of that is stiff upper lip and all, but a good chunk is simply that Maggie was someone they really didn't know. I didn't either, though I lived right next door.

If Maggie wouldn't stop staring at me, Sonny would never look at me. I thought he was just unsocial. A conversation finally began when I came out and asked him where he got the stones he was using for his wall.

The pile of rocks is Sonny's work too. It's not made

up of discarded headstones smashed up out of respect for the delicate sensibilities of the dead. His raw materials are a combination of fieldstones, bedrock and discarded chunks of granite. When you dig up a plot, rocks turn up. They must be removed. It's not that different from tilling soil for crops, except the coffins going into the ground are never meant to grow.

The task of building a wall wants good, longish, flat stones of high quality, not crap rubble made of plaster and cement mixed with gravel. He's found good stones and hauled them to his spot, dumping them out of his pickup and spreading them around as the dust flies up, covering him with a fine white powder that gets in his ears, up his nose, makes him cough.

"Used to smoke," he tells me. Quit after the cancer started up in his lungs.

To the naked eye he looks positively robust for a man of 80-odd years who survived on account of cussed stubbornness and not much else. He got experimental treatment at the VA, turning him into a walking cocktail of elixirs and drugs keeping death at bay. It's a miracle he gets out of bed, but he does, building this wall, moving stones, ton by ton.

He's a veteran of the Korean War. I'm Korean. He didn't know what to say to me. Thankfully, he didn't try the little bit of the language he used to use to pick up girls in Seoul. He's not the chatty type. The wall is his sermon. His apology to the child he wished he had instead of the one he actually did.

His son's a disappointment. In and out of jail. Vandalized John's car. Sonny didn't know what to say to him.

"It's like a three dimensional puzzle," I say. "Your wall, I mean. You probably don't know what Tetris is, but it's like that, fitting the pieces together, figuring out where they're supposed to go."

"It's not so hard," he mumbles. "You have to watch the cracks. Do some chinking as it goes."

"I'd ask you to teach me," I joke, "but those things are too heavy for me to lift."

He eyeballs me, confused. Breaking stones with a sledgehammer is not the kind of thing that small women generally take up as a hobby.

His wife is a recluse who became an invalid. She's sick.

Of what? I don't know. Of life, I guess.

"It's beautiful," I say seriously. "Your wall is a work of art."

"It's almost finished," he mumbles. Embarrassed, he turns away, and resumes carrying his heavy, heavy stones.

John comes home with an armful of tiger lilies in fresh bloom.

"I took them from Maggie's lawn," he says. "I don't think she'd mind."

Maggie's house is rapidly turning to mush, reminding me of a very large dead elephant decomposing in high temperatures. The front lawn is turning into a jungle of grasses too tall for the small patch of lawn. The short path to her door is being swallowed up by weeds. While she was alive, she didn't do much to keep the place in order. Now that she's gone, the overgrowth has sped up. Her sisters have returned to England, and junk mail is accumulating.

You'd be surprised how often mail doesn't get forwarded when the recipient is deceased.

It's already dark when two police cars pull up and stop at Maggie's house. They pull out flashlights, go into the house and start poking around. The lights move, shining out through broken windows. Curious, I go outside to ask the officers why they'd decided to investigate.

"Someone reported that the door was open," the first officer replies flatly. He sounds like Detective Friday on *Dragnet*.

"It's always open," I say, shrugging. "The door doesn't close."

"How long has it been open?" the officer asks.

"It's always open," I repeat, "because it won't shut. Uh—you do know that the owner died?"

A second officer emerges from the house and joins the conversation. "She's right. The door won't close. It doesn't fit in the frame."

The foundation's cracked. The house settled. So the windows won't open, and the doors won't close.

"The front door didn't close when she was alive," I tell them. "It's not like it's going to fix itself now."

The two of them stare at me as if I'm a talking owl. In the back of my head I'm trying to figure out who would have called the police about the door, and decide, irrationally, that it's one of the dog walkers always coming back here so their pooches can swim in the pond.

"Besides which," I add brightly, "you guys went inside. There's nothing in there worth stealing."

Neither of them crack a smile. They are very serious, with shaved heads and the look of men who used to be in the military. With shaved heads like Sonny's.

"OK," they say in unison. "We'll make sure the town knows about the death, and hopefully whoever's in charge of the house will take care of it."

They drive away. The door stays open.

Sonny's wall is nearly done. It's a foot thick, each stone in the right place, no signs of leaking or fissures. The last bit of wall is the topping. The corners are strong.

The wall isn't finished. But I haven't seen Sonny for a while.

When the ambulances came, I wondered. But it wasn't for Sonny. It was for his wife.

Because she died at home, her body had to be autopsied. It didn't matter that she was very old and sick for years. She died in her own bed, and that makes the circumstances irregular. It's just not done. Not any more.

It was The Jerk's kids who told me. They hate me but love Sonny. Now that he doesn't have his wife to look after, they are trying to look out for him. They've been bringing him beer and chips, you know, stuff to eat. Their faces are earnest as they smoke nervously, having come to the wall to chat with the enemy.

"That's some wall Sonny's built for you," I say quietly.

"We know," they reply, and take long, deep drags, the kind that kill time with every breath.

Because they've watched him too, young boys with strong backs and weak wills. It's finally dawned on them what patience can do. It can create an object strong enough to withstand death. To their teenage minds, an impossibility filled with romance. Fuck yeah. He's cool.

I bring Sonny a lasagna and a loaf of homemade bread. He doesn't answer the door, so I leave it on his stoop. I don't leave a note. He will know who it is from.

A few weeks later, it's pouring rain, the kind of drenching storm that drives earthworms out of their holes, lest the water fill their homes and they drown. I look out my kitchen window, and through the heavy drops I can make out a man, walking back and forth, the water a veil turning him into a ghost. It's Sonny, back at work, finishing his wall. One gravestone at a time.

Four Days Forever
J.J. Hensley

Friday

A shotgun is a formidable weapon. The pain from the impact in my torso reminds me of that fact. It is also a simple weapon, which can be made ready to fire in one deliberate motion and then discharged with a simple pull of the trigger. Assuming the safety switch is in the correct position, what follows is deafening and eternal. Along with the smoke, the scent of discharged rage fills the living room of this duplex on the east side of Pittsburgh. The neighbors will dial 9-1-1, and the cops and EMTs will try to keep the response time under five minutes. As the effects radiate through me, I realize the cops and medics don't matter because I'll be gone.

In a split second, past decisions became today's consequences. All of this may seem sudden, but it's the end of a longer road that had been lined with warning signs. People sometimes see a lightning bolt and forget it's the knifepoint of what was once a slow, momentum-building storm. I suppose a personal apocalypse is never as sudden as it seems. Somewhere in days past, a fuse was lit and actions began demanding reactions.

Yes, a shotgun is a formidable weapon.

24 hours earlier
Thursday

I heard it in Jerrod's voice when he cancelled on me.

"Can we go some other time? I've got this project for school, and it's due tomorrow."

"Sure," I said.

His words were fine, but the tone was wrong. When you come from a family of hard men saying hard things while drinking hard liquor, the tiniest hints of sorrow or regret stand out like wounds waiting to be drowned in salt. We build up psychological and emotional walls—it's what we do. You have to shape and fortify these walls because the kinds of people you deal with are quick to exploit any exposed cracks in your disposition and transform them into scars on your face.

"We can go tomorrow and get something to eat on the way," I suggested.

He paused a beat too long before answering, "Yeah, let's do that. I'll call you tomorrow, OK?"

"Sure," I said again before hanging up and grabbing my keys.

I'm not accustomed to following my younger brother around. Even at the age of 16, he's pretty good at looking out for himself.

When I was his age, Mom was already long gone, and Pop was spending his nights pounding on deadbeats for a bookie and his days pounding on me. Jerrod managed to avoid much of the violence, and that was OK as far as I was concerned.

I'd like to think the reason he dodged some of the smacks was because I would do my best to make sure the back of Pop's hand found my face rather than my brother's. But the truth is Jerrod has always had a way about him. He's smart, and not just street smart like Pop and me. Jerrod's got that spark that threatens run-of-the-mill degenerates. The small-time punks get insecure when they see some kid might be able to do more than break thumbs or run a short con.

Those guys are a hassle, but it's the *real* players who are the threat to my brother. To the players, the spark is intriguing because they see a kid who rose above being an alcoholic knuckle-dragging thug like his father and can become more than a respected, but relatively small-time, operator like his older brother.

If Jerrod has one weakness, it's that he's not a great liar. That's why I knew something was up when he cancelled on me for the movies.

I was never great in school, but Jerrod's always been a good student and he's talked about college. When I was old enough to defend myself against Pop, I made it clear that Jerrod would be getting an education and making a decent name for himself. But last April, on my 20th birthday, Pop had suggested taking Jerrod on a collection job.

"It's just to show him how the world works," he said. "I did the same thing when you were his age, and you turned out all right."

That was when, without a second of hesitation, I slugged my father in the gut. Pop never brought up the idea again.

Looking back now, I remember glancing at my brother while Pop tried to catch his breath. I've been trying to tell myself Jerrod's expression was one of disbelief, but now I suspect something different and dangerous had been dwelling underneath the surprise. Had there been a trace of disappointment in his face?

After the punch, Pop had tried to straighten up and

play it tough, but then I reminded him about the promise I had made two days prior. That's when I saw the fear deep behind his eyes—it was something I'd never seen in him before.

The crack in his wall was visible, and he knew what I'd do if I found out he was dragging Jerrod into the gutter.

Nobody makes a postcard of Pittsburgh in November. The chill of the rain hits your bones and sticks with you until March. Windshields fog and blur, the lines on the road fade into the asphalt, and the last thing anyone thinks about is to check for a tail. I watched Jerrod come out of the house and start up Pop's old Buick. My heart sank when Pop slinked into the passenger seat before the car pulled out into the evening traffic. I followed them down Penn Avenue and then paralleled them as they took secondary streets into Forest Hills. I lost them for a few minutes when I got caught at a light, but then I noticed the Buick in the parking lot of a fast food restaurant.

Finding an inconspicuous spot in an office complex down the street, I parked and shut off the lights of my Dodge. At a diagonal angle, I watched the Buick, the occasional passing headlights revealing two people in the car. The Buick had been backed into a spot in the manner with which I was all too familiar. My mind flashed back to when I was 16 and driving that car with Pop sitting beside me, teaching me the finer points of casing a place we would hit a couple of days later.

As I watched blue exhaust drift up from behind the Buick, my hands strangled the steering wheel. After a while, Jerrod and Pop pulled away, and I waited 10 minutes before backing my car into the spot that had been vacated. My wipers swept away waves of water long

enough for me to see a gold exchange shop on the corner
of a strip mall. Not a high-end jewelry store that carries a
lot of diamonds or anything like that. Nope. Pop was
having Jerrod help him rob what was nothing more than
a fucking pawn shop on steroids.

"Idiot!" I said aloud as I pounded the top of the
wheel. After receiving the gut punch on my birthday, Pop
had sworn to keep Jerrod out of the business. No cons,
no collections and certainly no strong-arm jobs. Now
that idiot was looking to get my brother shot or locked
up by holding up some nickel-and-dime gold exchange.
And for what kind of take? A few thousand in cash—*if*
they could get in the safe. They would undoubtedly pull a
smash and grab, and pick up some jewelry while the
alarms blared in the background. They'd wear masks, but
cameras were all over those joints, and even the slightest
shred of evidence can give the cops probable cause when
dealing with people like us.

I shouldn't have been surprised, because Jerrod's
behavior had changed over the past year. He talked less
about school and got in more fights. It's to be expected.
When you are drowning in the life, it's only so long until
you have to take some short breaths. But this job was a
deep swallow in murky waters. I had promised my
brother I'd look out for him and keep him straight. Pop
had promised to not steer Jerrod wrong. Promises must
be kept.

48 hours earlier
Wednesday

"Two thousand is the best I can do," said Marcus
from behind the card table he called a desk.

It was always the same routine with him. He'd try to
lowball me, and I'd get the price worked up to within 10
percent of the asking price. Going through this dog and

pony show every time with your fence is annoying as hell, but as long as you get close to your asking price you stick with people you trust.

I leaned back in my chair. "I got this stuff from a score in the North Hills, not a flea market. Thirty-two hundred and I'll have something else for you soon."

I was lying to him, and he knew it. No thief with any amount of sense advertises where he takes scores. This was the usual course of business for the back room of Riverside Pawn. Lies, stolen goods and cash—each having significant value—were exchanged along with words spoken in hushed tones.

"Maybe I can give you twenty-two," he said in a low voice, while glancing at a monitor to see if anyone was coming into the shop. "But unloading these coins isn't like getting rid of flat screens. The cops and insurance people will be looking for them to turn up."

"You know I know that, and you know how much they're really worth. I'm giving you a bargain price because you're going to have to sit on them or melt them. I don't really care."

Marcus smiled. "You're an odd man, Ray. You know that, don't you? You bring in great stuff but never want to shop it around for the big money. *Unload and cash out* seems to be your motto. You like the high-risk jobs but don't want to try for the high-risk money."

"It's my call," I said. "So you don't need to be talking to my father about our business, understand?"

He looked mildly ashamed and shrugged a fat shoulder.

"Three thousand," I said.

"Come on," Marcus smirked. "We've been doing business for years and with you that's all it is—all business. Throw me a bone."

I sighed. "What are you asking me, Marcus?"

He rubbed his chin, leaned forward and asked, "Why

do you risk taking hard-to-unload scores from places with complicated alarms and all that security, but you don't ever wait around for me to take bidders for the premium items?"

Having a personal relationship with your fence is never a good idea. I debated shutting him down, but the question struck something inside of me, and I felt compelled to answer, if only so he would stop gossiping on the street.

"You can circumvent alarm systems. You can run from a security guard. You can elude a patrol car. But you can never really keep a money trail from ending at your doorstep."

Marcus gave a nod, but then cocked his head and said, "Come on now, you and I both know people who can wash cash, and it comes out looking legit."

He was right. I wasn't big time, but I certainly had connections who knew how to launder money. That wasn't the issue.

"If I start thinking it's acceptable to wait one month for a big payoff, then I'll start thinking two months is fine."

"So?" Marcus asked.

"Then why not wait three months for an even bigger score?" I asked, rhetorically. "How about six months for six figures? Next thing you know, one of us is sitting on a painting or vase for a year and collecting bids from a dozen people we don't really know." I shook my head and concluded, "The exposure is too great."

The fence nodded, but I could see he wasn't sure if I was serious about my precautions. It's not that I couldn't do the time if I got busted. I'd been in and out of juvie since I was 14 and did a couple of stints in county as an adult, but I always had a lot of motivation to avoid hard time. Pop had been getting sloppier and sloppier over the past few years, and it was just a matter of time until he got pinched and sent away. What would become of Jerrod if I was in the cage too? No, Jerrod was going to be the break in the cycle. His spark wasn't going to be extinguished because of Pop getting careless or me getting greedy. Of course, I wasn't going to explain all of that to Marcus. My walls weren't going to show any cracks. My walls had to be fucking seamless.

"Here's three K," he said as he stuffed three thousand in 20s into an envelope.

We stood up, and I slid the envelope into my jacket. Our business concluded, he led me out of the back room and into the semi-legit portion of the pawn shop.

"Say 'hello' to your dad for me," said Marcus.

I nodded and took another three steps.

"And to your brother too," he added. "He's a good kid."

I stopped in my tracks and turned toward him as a chime sounded on the door, and a couple walked in carrying a box of junk they were undoubtedly looking to sell. Marcus immediately turned his attention to the customers and guided them to a counter where he would sort through the box and offer next-to-nothing cash for next-to-worthless trinkets.

I strode out onto the broken sidewalk and pulled my coat around me before turning and looking through the window of Marcus' shop. He saw me and gave me a final wave, and I thought about how careful I had always been to keep our relationship professional rather than personal.

Marcus knew me because of Pop and knew Pop because of the business, but that was where it ended. For all my father's faults, he knew how to separate the business side of things from most of the personal stuff. You don't talk to your fence about friends, plans, jobs and certainly not about family. You might prep your fence if you were expecting to bring in a score that needed to be moved fast, but that's about the only time you talk to him when you won't be walking out with cash in your pocket. There is simply no other reason to be there.

So, how the hell did Marcus know Jerrod? I'd have to call my brother and try to meet up with him. We needed to talk.

72 hours earlier
Tuesday

My family doesn't have many traditions, but I guess having a beer with your father in the living room is the closest thing we have to a ritual. I took a seat and noticed the hockey game flickering on the television. As usual, Pop grumbled about the Pens not playing up to his insane expectations. Pop had never laced up a pair of skates in his life, but over time he'd anointed himself a hockey expert. I grabbed a beer from the mini-fridge in the corner and took my usual seat. Pop barely glanced my way as I looked around the room, angling my head so I could see through the kitchen doorway.

"Where's Jerrod?" I asked.

Pop pointed up, letting me know my brother was in his room.

Minutes passed before he said, "I've been hearing things about you."

I didn't say anything. That's the thing about my father. If you stay quiet long enough, you can count on him filling the conversational void.

He shifted in his fake leather recliner and stroked an area patched with duct tape as he said, "The word is you've been making out real good on some jobs. Some people say you've been making out too good. Like you've been pulling jobs that attract attention but not getting paid like you should."

"Marcus talks too much," is all I said.

"It's not just him," said Pop. "Word is getting around. People are saying you're not being patient enough or maybe you've got a habit to feed and need the quick buck. You hooked on something?"

"No," I replied.

"So what's the problem?"

"You wouldn't understand," I said, and turned to pretend to watch the game.

I heard the chair groan under my father's weight as he leaned forward.

"I don't get you. You've got a decent head on your shoulders, and thanks to those technical classes you took, you know how to work alarms, cameras and fancy locks. But you don't have one bit of sense when it comes to the business. With your skills you could be raking it in with no problems. I know people who can handle the merchandise and get you a fair cut."

I took a sip of beer and tried to ignore him. I debated pointing out that he—with all his business sense—was still living in the same run-down house I'd grown up in and that he barely had a penny to his name, but we'd been down that road before. That conversational trail led to stories of imagined slights where he was the victim of bad deals, shady partners and poor advice. In reality, he was the generator of those deals, the partner who was shady and a terrible advisor. So I sat and drank my beer in silence.

"That's the difference between you and Jerrod," he said, getting my attention. "That kid's going places. By the time he's your age, he might be sending out his own crews to do the dirty work while he sits by a pool with a drink in one hand and a girl in the other. He's got a brain to go with the talent."

I put my bottle on the table and stood up.

"Pop, I'm going to make this very clear. If I find out

you've got Jerrod pulling any jobs or running any cons, here is what I'm going to do: I'm going to walk in here with a shotgun, I'm going to pull it tight to my shoulder, aim it at your chest and pull the trigger. Any pain I feel from the recoil against my shoulder will be the sweetest feeling in the world because I'll know I'll be handing Jerrod a real future. Things will end for Jerrod and me in this city, but for you—they'll end forever."

I made him that promise on a Tuesday in November. And promises must be kept.

Apfelstrudel
Vicki Lesage

"Give it back!" my younger brother screamed.

"No! It's mine!" his twin sister whined.

"I had it first!"

"I'm older!"

"By ten minutes. That doesn't even count."

My siblings, with light skin and mousy brown hair that matched mine, thought they were so grown-up. They'd been making noise and driving me crazy for four years now—not that I complained. As their older sister, I was too mature to gripe about such things. Whenever I needed to assert my authority, all 10 years of it, I reminded them that my age contained two digits. That shut them up real quick.

"Quiet, now!" Mother shouted from the kitchen. She was more effective than me, but couldn't always be relied on to get the job done.

These arguments between my brother and sister were nothing new, but something felt different at our house lately. Mother and Father whispered a lot. They thought we didn't notice, and Hans and Hannelore probably *didn't* notice, but I knew something was going on. I'd hear the occasional phrase and try to piece together the entire story. "Not a good sign" or "we need to leave" or "what about the children?"

What were they worried about? Maybe Father's job. He'd been spending less time at the office lately because he had fewer patients. Normally that would be a good thing—more time to spend with us and fewer sick people to take care of. But people were always sick, so it was odd that they weren't going to see him any more. The families from temple still went to him, but the rest had found new doctors. Why? Father never said.

Or maybe they were worried about money, which would make sense if Father's practice was failing. We always had food on the table, but I noticed the desserts were getting skimpy. Mother used to make this delicious *apfelstrudel* each Sunday, and if we ate small portions, we could make it last until Wednesday.

Oh how I loved her *apfelstrudel!* Grandmother had taught her how to make it just the way I liked it. Well, I guess it just so happened to be the way I liked it because Grandmother taught Mother long before I was born. It must have taken years to perfect the recipe. You could find *apfelstrudel* in every bakery, but none had the delicate, flaky crust that Mother's did. None had tender apples that melted in your mouth. None had the hint of spice... What spice was that? I didn't know. She had promised to teach me, but she hadn't had time yet. Maybe if she wasn't keeping so many secrets with Father she could have found an afternoon for me.

"Everyone get cleaned up for dinner. Quickly!" Mother called out from the doorway, then let the door swing back into place as she returned to her cooking.

I helped Hans and Hannelore so it wouldn't take all night. The sweet smell of *apfelstrudel* had wafted in from the kitchen, and I knew we were in for a treat. I wanted to hurry up and eat my plate of brisket so we could get to the good part. With dessert appearing less and less often, we had to enjoy it when we could.

"Stop pushing!" Hans cried as Hannelore shoved him off the worn wooden stepstool in front of the sink.

"Children!" I reprimanded, then reached my arms around them to wash my own hands. Seriously! They could be such babies.

As we arrived at the dinner table, Mother and Father abruptly stopped their conversation. Mother had a strange look on her face, the same one she used when she had told me we couldn't get a puppy, and the same one she used to break the news that Hannelore had torn the pages out of my favorite book. Something was definitely going on. Something bad. She hadn't burned the *apfelstrudel*, had she? No, I didn't detect anything other than the pleasant scent of baking apples in our cozy kitchen. Maybe our parents would finally explain what they had been whispering about?

"Children, sit down. We have to tell you something."

I knew it. Hannelore and Hans started arguing over who had more potatoes on their plates, but I watched Mother without saying a word.

"You're going to stay with some friends for a few days. A few towns over. You leave tonight. We will join you after the Sabbath. Father needs to finish some business, and you know he can't work late on Friday."

"Can I bring my train?" Hans asked.

"It's already packed, sweetie."

"How come he gets a train?" Hannelore wailed. "I want my dolly!" Of course.

"That's already packed, too, dear."

I didn't bother to ask what was packed for me. I didn't want to leave our house or my friends. I didn't know what was happening, but I knew it wasn't good.

Something told me we would be gone for longer than a few days.

"Eat up, children! There's *apfelstrudel* for dessert."

But I didn't want any. The sweet aroma I normally loved hung in the air, making me sick.

"Edith, where's Mama?" Hannelore asked, tapping my shoulder as I threw back the ratty blanket I'd been sleeping under.

"Shh, you'll wake Hans," I whispered.

"I'm already awake, Edith. I can't sleep. Where's Mama? Where's Papa?"

I couldn't show my fear, but I was as scared and worried as they were. The weekend had passed, and Mother and Father hadn't come. The friends we were staying with had been nice enough, but they made us hide in the cellar and the three of us had to sleep on one mattress. We knew them simply as "Madame" and "Monsieur." They fed us weird food I couldn't even pronounce. The worst was *tarte Tatin*, a poor excuse for Mother's *apfelstrudel*. Living in a basement should have been the bigger part of my worries, but something about the dessert struck me. It was as if this couple was trying to reassure us everything was OK when it clearly wasn't. And that meant things must be even worse than we realized.

"Go back to sleep, children. If Mother and Father said they were coming, they're coming."

Two more weeks passed, and Mother and Father never came. Madame and Monsieur let us out of the cellar for 30 minutes each day so we could run around their yard and breathe fresh air. But then we had to go back and hide. Hans and Hannelore would play while I sat under an apple tree in their back yard, trying not to cry about all I had left behind. What were my friends doing? What was I missing in school?

Madame and Monsieur weren't Jewish so we hadn't been to temple since we left home. I admit I didn't really mind—I much preferred reading or spending time alone—but all their books were in French, and I was getting bored. Well, as bored as you can get when you're scared out of your mind.

"*Allez les enfants*, back to your room."

"It's not a room, it's a cave," Hannelore said. "When can we leave? We don't want to stay in this stupid cave any more! Where's Mama?" Her lip quivered, and I knew she was about to cry.

"Shh, child," Madame murmured as she ushered us down the rickety steps. "You will be able to leave soon."

We heard the distinctive click of the lock and knew we were in for the night.

"Quickly, quickly!" Monsieur's voice roused us from our sleep. Except for the flashlight he held, it was pitch black in our cellar. It must have still been nighttime. "It's time to leave."

"Leave?" Hans said. "Are Mama and Papa here?"

"Finally!" Hannelore shouted. "Mama and Papa are here!"

But I knew they weren't. If they were, they would be here with us now. No, something even worse was happening.

"Come, now," Monsieur insisted.

He led us up the stairs and nudged us into the backseat of a car, where the door had been open, waiting for us. Once we were inside, he slammed the door and tapped the roof of the car. The driver sped off down the dirt road, past an odd-looking statue of a cat and into the blackness of the night.

"*Je suis désolé, je ne parle pas allemand,*" he said. I had studied a little French in school, enough to understand that he had said he didn't speak German. He didn't say anything else the entire drive.

"Try to sleep, children," I said to Hans and Hannelore.

They huddled up against me and drifted off to sleep. I eventually fell asleep myself, my face pressed against the cool glass of the car window.

When we woke up, we were surrounded by the most beautiful buildings I'd ever seen. This city must have been a million times larger than the tiny town we were from and the tiny village we'd been hiding in for the past few weeks.

The sun was rising. We must have driven all night.

The driver opened the back door. "*Dépêchez-vous,*" he ordered, motioning with his hand for us to exit.

"Hurry, children," I said. I turned back to grab our suitcases, but it was only then that I realized our bags weren't with us. We'd left so fast we hadn't even gotten to take our belongings.

"*Un café crème, s'il vous plaît,*" I said to the waiter as I sat down at the corner café. Ten years of living in Paris and I'd nearly perfected my accent. It helped that I'd learned it so young.

Hans and Hannelore were even better. If you didn't know otherwise—if you didn't know that we came from a German village right across the French border—you'd think we were all Parisian.

We'd adapted quickly to our new life. The city was wonderful, and the couple who took us in was welcoming. They'd enrolled us in school and gave us intense French lessons every spare minute. They told us to only speak French in public and in private—to never let anyone hear us speak German. We still did, though, when it was just the three of us, settling into bed at night.

We went to church every Sunday, and I always thought to myself that Mother would kill us if she found out. But of course she never would find out. Because we never saw her again. Not Father, either.

At the time, we were too young to know the details. We thought our parents had abandoned us. Once the adults stopped whispering behind our backs and started talking to us, and once our French became fluent enough, we learned of the Great War. We learned of a man who hated us, even though he didn't know us. We learned that Mother and Father had sent us away to save us. But we didn't learn what happened to Mother and Father.

Now, as I sat in a café along Boulevard Haussmann, I thought back to those first few weeks. How living in that cellar felt like torture of the worst kind. Ha! If I'd only known. I'd read about the torture innocent people—my people—had suffered, and it was infinitely worse than what we'd gone through. It was all so senseless and cruel.

Why had we been allowed to escape while others hadn't?

Guilt about this overwhelmed me. I guess I really had converted to Catholicism, hadn't I? I at least had the guilt part down. I sipped my coffee without enjoying it.

My brother, my sister and I had survived. Mother and Father hadn't. I tried to appreciate my new life. I knew I should be grateful for it. But I missed Mother and Father so badly. I didn't have a single memento. Not even a tiny scrap from my previous life to hold on to…

But wait! The luggage! We had left our bags behind in the cold, damp cave because we'd departed in such a hurry. I wondered: *Now—now that the war was over, and we could travel freely—could I return to that country house and retrieve our belongings? And thank Monsieur and Madame for saving us?*

I was afraid to face the past but exhilarated at the same time. I'd hardly thought about that cellar during the past decade, and now I couldn't get it out of my mind.

I stepped off the train and glanced around, hoping to recognize something in the small French town, so small that its "station" was a lone shack next to the tracks. I could see the village square from here, but of course it didn't look familiar. I hadn't ever seen the actual town before. I'd barely seen more than the house we'd stayed in and the narrow dirt road taking us to our new life.

I entered the station and studied a tattered map affixed to the wall. That's when it hit me how foolish I'd been to come here on such little information. Monsieur and Madame hadn't even told us their names! Hans and Hannelore (or Henri and Hannah as they went by now) were in school back in Paris so I'd have to figure this out on my own.

I headed to the main plaza and wandered into one of the cafés that lined the square. "*Un café crème, s'il vous plaît.*" My usual.

"You are not from around here, Mademoiselle?" the waiter asked. Not impolite, just curious.

"Is it obvious?"

"Your accent, the way you dress, and the fact I saw you get off the train," he said with a wink. "And your luggage."

Oh, yes. My luggage. "I'm from Paris, but I'm here to find some old family friends. Perhaps you can help?"

"I can certainly try. What is their name?"

"I don't know."

"Where do they live?"

"I don't know."

"What do they do?"

"I don't know."

"Mademoiselle, I would love to help you, but I am not a magician."

I stirred some sugar into my coffee, realizing how ridiculous I must have looked. He was about to walk away, when it hit me. "Wait! I think they were apple farmers. I remember sitting under an apple tree in their orchard, and they always served us *tarte Tatin*."

"That's a start, but there are many apple farmers in the area. Do you remember anything else?"

"They lived off a long dirt road… Oh, and they had a peculiar statue of a cat in their front yard."

"Oh yes! Madame and Monsieur Bernard. Everyone knows them by that hideous statue. And their famous *tarte Tatin*. Let me show you their address on a map."

The country house was a good 30-minute walk from the town center, but I was energized from the coffee. And from the thought of being so close to such a distant part of my past.

My shoes were covered in a thin layer of dust from the unpaved road, and my feet ached, but I didn't care. When I passed the cat statue, I knew I was in the right place. I walked up the pathway to the front door and paused. Was I ready to face my past? Would these people react kindly to me appearing on their doorstep? Maybe this hadn't been such a good idea after all.

"Are you going to knock, or do you plan to stand there all day?" a voice asked from behind me.

I turned to see a thin middle-aged woman with a smile on her face, gardening gloves covering her hands and dirt covering her apron.

"I'm sorry. Madame Bernard?" My heart was beating a mile a minute. I had dreamed of this moment since that day in the café, yet I hadn't actually planned what I would say. What could I say? Thoughts jumbled in my head, but before I could decide where to start, a spark of recognition shined in the woman's eyes.

"The beautiful Edith! Is it really you?"

I nodded, grateful for those words, grateful I wouldn't have to explain the whole painful story from the beginning.

"I recognize you, my dear. And I suppose I'm not really surprised... I always knew you would return. Come, let's go inside and have a tea, shall we?"

For the first time, I entered the cottage. During the three weeks we spent in the cellar, I'd always wondered what the house was like. What the people who lived there were like.

"Help yourself to a pastry while I get the tea on," Madame said.

I looked around the house, and memories flooded my mind. It felt so bizarre since I'd never been in those rooms before. Yet the sounds and smells were familiar. Again, my heart raced as I remembered the panic I'd felt all those years ago. Trying to remain calm so as not to scare the twins, yet being terrified myself.

"I imagine you have some questions for me," Madame said, setting a teacup on the table.

"I do," I replied, cradling the warm cup in my hands. "I've managed to piece a lot together over the years. I... thank you. Thank you for helping us. For saving us. It was a huge risk for you."

"Oh, it was nothing." She smiled and let out a tiny laugh. "Actually, no, it was not nothing. It was the most frightening thing we'd ever done. But you don't have to thank me. It's what you do. You help people, you know?"

"Did you ever hear what happened to my parents?"

She paused and looked down at her teacup. She ran a finger along the edge of the saucer, then stopped. She looked up and said simply, "No."

That "no" weighed a thousand kilos. I suspected she

knew much more than she let on. I also suspected it was something I was not ready to hear. Not yet. Maybe I would gain the courage to ask her one day, or maybe I would find my answers elsewhere. Today, I had a different goal.

"I don't have anything from my parents, anything physical. Not a single memento. Our suitcases... Do you by chance still have them?"

The country house was charming but tidy. Would she have tossed out the suitcases, figuring she had no need for them? Or would she have saved them, wanting a memento herself of the surreal time she had helped three German children escape certain death?

"I don't know why, but yes, I have saved them. Help yourself to more tea. I'll be right back."

I glanced around the kitchen as I waited. But the shelves lined with jars of flour, sugar and various baking pans weren't enough to distract me. What would I find in the suitcases? What was I even hoping to find?

Madame returned with the luggage. Three small trunks. "I'm sorry, I should have offered to help," I said, heat rising to my cheeks.

"*Non, non,* you're a guest. Which one is yours?" I pointed to the largest of the three. "We'll start with that one." She carried it over and set it at my feet.

I hesitated, then thrust it open. A musty scent filled the kitchen as I sifted through my long-forgotten belongings. Books, of course, along with my favorite dress, some other clothes. All *my* things but nothing from Mother.

"Thank you," I managed to say. But I wanted to cry. I'd come here to revisit my past and hopefully find a souvenir. This suitcase would have to be enough. The memory that Mother had lovingly packed these items for me, knowing she was sending me off to a better life, and knowing she was not likely to see me again. Any of us.

As I pushed the trunk off to the side, a piece of paper slipped out and fluttered to the stone floor. How had I missed that?

"What's that, my dear?"

"I don't know," I replied, reaching for the note. I unfolded it, recognizing Mother's slanted writing immediately. Tears welled up in my eyes, and a smile slowly stretched across my face.

"What is it?"

"It's Mother's recipe for *apfelstrudel*. She knew it was my favorite. She had been about to teach me how to make it before..." I choked on my words and couldn't get the rest out.

Madame rose from her chair, walked around behind me and placed her arms on my shoulders. "It seems you have found what you were looking for. Stay here for a few days. Maybe we can discover this recipe together."

I looked out the kitchen window to the orchard and thought back to all the *tartes Tatin* this kind woman had made for me and how I'd never appreciated them. And how, ever since, I couldn't eat apple tart because it brought back too many painful memories. And I looked at the scrap of paper with my mother's handwriting, the only thing left of her in this world.

"Yes, that sounds lovely," I said. My heart ached for my mother, yet I felt something else as well. Hope. Hope that baking this silly dessert would help me remember my mother, my former life. That maybe, just maybe, it would finally taste sweet again.

Nagasaki
David Whitehouse

In the 1920s, when Choko was small, she adored the life-sized tigers her father painted on the sliding paper doors that separated the tatami rooms at home. He was a coal miner, and the family lived on the Takashima mining island off the west coast of Nagasaki peninsula in southern Japan.

When Choko was a teenager, she started to take part in the island's annual summer festival. She was one of the girls who each July donned bright blue kimonos and struggled through the humid evening in their wooden sandals with the rest of the procession.

The air would be smoky and damp, loaded with the smell of grilled fish. The men would carry a huge painted plaster dragon, mounted on a wooden pallet, on their shoulders. If it rained, the kimonos with their red sashes would get wetter and more revealing, and the girls would dance more keenly to the cacophony of beating drums and clanging bells.

One year, as she danced, a tiny needle of light in her

mind told her there would be trouble. The same sliver of light had soundlessly intimated the year before that her brother would come home from school camp in the mainland mountains with a broken arm.

When the procession finished, she told her father she wanted him to take her home. He wouldn't listen and kept drinking beer in the village square with the rest of the men. Their songs got louder and cruder. Then she saw him with the shiny red eye of the dragon in his hands, trying to thrust it under his coat. He was a poor man, and the eye could be sold for at least a month's wages.

Then he was down in the mud, and she could see the crowd of men kicking, kicking him again and again until the eye slipped from his hands and into the mud. She pushed against the mob to reach him, but she couldn't get through. No one heard her as she screamed at them to stop. Choko's father died from his injuries within a few days.

Ten years later, in 1937, Japanese soldiers invaded China and occupied the city of Shanghai. Choko was still living in Takashima with her now elderly mother. Her brother had married and moved to another village. The tigers on the doors, which had been as large as life, were now shrunken and faded, and marked by dirty fingerprints.

The soldiers came to the house and seized her. They wanted to use her to stop Japanese troops raping their way indiscriminately across the eastern Chinese seaboard, which would have inflamed local resistance to the occupation. They wanted her to control China. With her body she was to hold the Chinese at bay for her masters.

They shipped her there and gave her a tatty gray kimono. She lived in a tiny hut that had insects crawling on the floor. As she was raped every day, 10 times a day or even more, sometimes by two at once, she began to concentrate on the tiny needle of light that still existed in her mind.

As Choko concentrated on it, the eye of the needle became a little wider and seemed to become a tunnel that was inviting her to enter. Each day with the brutes inside her she would crawl a little further along the tunnel. One day the tunnel expanded, and she was able to stand up. There seemed to be something solid under her. She pressed down with the soles of her feet and was able to rock back and forth. She looked down, and she could see the brutes down there, and she suddenly felt that they were fucking a corpse.

She could also see outside the hut, the slack-jawed, unshaven soldiers smoking and waiting their turn. The tunnel opened out endlessly before her. She stepped forward into the light and was gone.

On the plane to Japan, the children were served first, but they fell asleep. Their trays of food sat untouched in front of them. I started on my holiday reading material by the Japanese writer Yukio Mishima. Would you like to be spun round in a fairground teacup? Mishima answered his own question with a definite *No*. Having written the final page of the four-book *Sea of Fertility* saga, Mishima in 1970 attempted to lead a military coup d'état which he hoped would restore traditional Japanese values. As he seems to have suspected, the soldiers who he incited to insurrection just laughed at him. He then committed ritual suicide at age 45.

I struggled with the first of the four books for a while but kept losing the threads of the reincarnation-based plot. Who was supposed to have been reborn as whom? The children were still asleep, and the economy-class food service for adults was miles away. Hungry passengers stared in disapproval as I demolished a child burger.

We changed planes in Seoul as it's the easiest way to get to Fukuoka on the southern Japanese island of Kyushu. One day to recover from the flight and then it was out into the post-modern consumerist wonderland. We started early in the morning. The drive from the wooden-framed house near Fukuoka city took about three hours. The group comprised my wife, our kids and my wife's extended family. There were nephews, nieces, cousins. They were all Japanese, and I was the only foreigner.

As we drove, I patiently lectured our callow audience about the historical influence of Catholic missionaries in southern Japan. After a while, the children began to doze. We stopped at a service station for breakfast. After we had eaten, I stood outside and stared at some kanji, complex Chinese pictographs that number in the thousands. These were imported into Japan in ancient times, and in a kind of linguistic skin transplant, grafted on to the existing spoken language. It's like writing English using Arab letters or whatever. I call it state-engineered dyslexia. The Koreans and the Vietnamese were sensible enough to drop them and come up with something easier, but the Japanese have persisted. Each kanji has its own meaning, as well as a variety of possible pronunciations; Japanese sounds for basic nouns, Chinese ones for more abstract compounds.

I stared at a group of three of these letters that seemed suddenly to swim together to give a rare glimpse of clarity.

"Life...science...application!" I turned to my wife in triumph. I was sure she would be pleased with my progress. "So that must be the drug store, right? But how do you pronounce it?"

"It means female hygiene," she said, slapping me on the arm. "Don't stand there with your mouth open.

Hurry up, will you, everyone's waiting!"

We headed on toward Nagasaki. We were soon there and found ourselves jammed in among the almost vertical slopes. The houses seemed to cling like limpets to the sides of a rock face. This is not a good place to ride a bike. Or buy a piano. Or get old.

To be fair, the locals' English didn't seem to be much better than my Japanese. For example: *Meat Is the King of Material.* What the hell was that supposed to mean? The sign was outside a butcher's shop and was presumably intended to attract customers from the local American military base.

Our next stop was the reconstructed Dutch trading settlement at Dejima. For the two centuries that ended in the 1850s, this was the country's only point of contact with the outside world. As we strolled around, I decided that the Protestant Dutch merchants had been much more sensible than the Catholics in Japan. Not only did they avoid being thrown into boiling water—always a risk for an overzealous missionary—but they were housed in spacious tatami-floored homes during their annual trading visits. These had now been restored and opened to the public.

The Japanese prized the silk and spices that the Dutch brought, and so hand-picked women from the city were made available to entertain them. In fact, these women were the only locals allowed into contact with the Dutch: You really needed a good reason to be let into the settlement. The term "Dutch wife" is still used nowadays in Japanese. These days it means "blow up doll."

I sat on the tatami and imagined myself as a Dutch merchant chilling out in a high-security comfort zone. As I daydreamed, one of our children charged across a carefully restored dining room. An alarm went off, and a security guard came running. I wrestled the kid back under control. The sweat glowed on the guard's neck as he wagged a white-gloved finger at me.

From Dejima, our ragged, floppy-hatted army toiled uphill through the afternoon humidity. We were bound for the Church of the Twenty-Six Martyrs, built in remembrance of a mixed group of Japanese and foreigners who were crucified for preaching Catholicism. It struck me as we climbed that the hill was a worse-than-average place to get crucified.

I have always been agnostic, at least since the long-ago night when a German student of philosophy pounded on a beer-soaked table in a furious response to my confident declaration of atheism. He told me I was *unlogisch*; the existence of God could not be proved or disproved either way. I decided that I couldn't argue with him. But how was I to label myself? Thomas Huxley, finding himself similarly confused a century earlier, had coined the term "agnostic" so that he might have "a tail like all the other foxes." That, I decided, would have to do.

In the toilets outside the church, a small boy in our group relieved himself squarely on my light tan trousers. I sighed and led him back to the group.

Inside the church, it was a surprise to find that the floor was flat and not sloping uphill toward the altar. That must have been some feat of construction. I sat in one of the pews and thought about the butcher's shop sign. Meat, the material king. The reason the sign here seemed so weird, I reckoned, was because in the west we like things to be capable of moving—like a person—before we start calling them the king of this, the king of that. Or start worshipping them as gods, for that matter. We like to see something that we can imagine as a proof of human control if we try hard enough. At home we have McDonald's or Burger King, but the king is not the meat itself. It's a human figure. It's either some Colonel Sanders-type guy lurking in the background, or the staff, collectively, or the customers, who are the kings.

The Japanese Shintoists, on the other hand, don't care about whether something can move or looks like a person. They don't need the illusion of human control. Nature is a law unto itself. They worship stones, the wind, the sun, mountains, waterfalls. It's the agnostic creed par excellence. There's hardly anything in the way of fixed belief, but an endless array of natural spirits to cut out and keep.

"Are we going to the hotel now?" I asked my wife. I wanted and deserved fresh trousers, dinner, beer. My leg was warm and damp, and it wasn't even my own kid who had done it.

"No," she said. "We're going to the atomic bomb museum."

I sighed. I had been there before. I remembered how the American pilots, blinded by the cloudy weather, had been just about to return to base. At the last moment, a brief chink of blue in the clouds; then mangled clocks stuck forever at 11:02 a.m.

"I'm tired," I said. "He pissed on me." I showed her the stain on my trousers. I pointed at the culprit.

"It'll be good for the children," she said. "We agreed, remember? You can change your trousers later. Come on." We collected our strength and ran down the hill in the gathering shadows of late afternoon.

How to Raise Cats in a Paris Apartment

Lizzie Harwood

It started with the mouse that scurried into our apartment. We were on the couch, enjoying *24 Season 3* mere days after moving into our new home.

Our building had been offices, now converted into 20 flats—shells—for their new owners to divvy into rooms and finish. We had our walls, courtesy of a guy called Fernando with a team of Eritrean laborers. The bathroom was tiled and done, but the rest of the 80 square meters was rough: no kitchen or doors, like some industrial private club. We had furniture, but bare concrete. And the front door had a three-centimeter gap to allow for flooring. The mouse cleared that no problem.

Only the woman across the hall had dared move in as quickly. We'd panicked about paying rent plus the mortgage and figured we'd finish things off on weekends, no sweat. My husband, MG, actually wrote "Kitchen: three days" on his planning schedule. It took him 21.

(The Eritreans had constructed unsquare walls.)

So I jumped up on the corner of the couch, screaming at the mouse. She wasn't big, but boy was she fast. She looked to be after the dregs of our Chinese takeaway but astonished at the hulking IKEA couch, glass table rising out of the concrete like an iceberg and metropolis of unpacked boxes. This was some nether region of do-it-yourself purgatory: a coven of construction tools, stacks of parquet still wrapped in plastic and an island of IKEA flat-packed goodies.

She stopped dead. Perhaps MG could've caught her in his bare hands if he'd had that instinct, but he was still setting down his glass of wine. I bent myself into a pretzel, squealing at the furry intruder to get the hell out. But instead of leaving, she scooted into the alcove where the dryer piggybacked atop the washing machine. And she was never seen again. Or, well, not for a long time.

Obviously, we had to get a cat. Immediately.

And if we got one, why not two? They could have company.

By some incredible coincidence, a secretary at work had a kitten needing a home. Céline was from a town near Amiens, nestled between the chilling First World War cemeteries, and her dad's cat had given birth to three kittens nobody wanted. Céline couldn't take any because she already had a cat—a deaf white tomcat she'd found in Greece and snuck home in her handbag on an Air France flight.

In the photo, one whiskered face stood out. Taupo. White with patches of peach tabby fur. Yellow eyes. *Adorable.*

"When can you bring her down?"

"I visit my dad every weekend. He's so depressed since my mother died."

Taupo's birth family was marked by tragedy: the widower who couldn't get organized to get the cat spayed, a sister still at home who wouldn't work and required financial propping up, and scant weeks after Taupo came to live with us, her mother and siblings died of cat flu. She was an orphan in every sense.

Céline brought her round on a Tuesday night. I had all the kitten gear ready. Among the takeout menus and power tools.

Meanwhile, one of MG's school friends had a kitten available in Brittany. Krakatoa's mummy, Petite Chatte, had delivered a boy and a girl. But the boy was a nasty piece of business, hissing at his litter-mate and generally hogging the best teat at every meal. Little green-eyed calico Krakatoa needed the love.

Yes, we named them after volcanoes. Taupo, short for Taupō-nui-a-Tia in New Zealand, is a caldera left after ancient catastrophic eruptions. And over in Indonesia, Krakatoa's 1883 explosions were heard in Rome and killed 36,000 people with the resulting tsunami. I came up with the idea. In retrospect, it wasn't a good one.

They got along beautifully. They slept in a violet glass fruit bowl on the dining table. You couldn't see where one cat began and the other ended. They spooned at the end of our bed at night. We doted. I took, oh, about 1,001 photos of them. "Works of art," bemused friends humored me, when I shoved cat photos in front of them. I fed the cats veterinary-approved cat biscuits and spoonfuls of tuna (in water, not oil!) because I wanted them to grow up with strong, healthy teeth and claws.

MG, on about Day 19 of his kitchen-construction lunacy (why, in God's name didn't we just get IKEA to install?), fashioned a feeding platform out of a leftover glossy red door panel suspended on poles above the deluxe 50-euro cat litter box with its Italian carbon filters for optimal ventilation.

Taupo would lie on the feeding platform, lazily inhaling *croquettes* that she swallowed without chewing, lapping Evian from a glass (they refused plastic). We noticed it was Kraki who actually cleaned Taupo. Either too indolent to lick herself, or too traumatized by the early loss of her mother and siblings, she didn't have a handle on grooming. So, Kraki did the dirty work, or Taupo dunked her head under the bathroom tap. I'd be at the sink, readying to insert contact lenses, and this white-and-orange blur would leap in to gulch and bat at the trickle. I took about 100 photos of that, too.

We vaccinated, of course, like good parents. Our vets were a couple of sharp men down on rue Etienne Marcel, who tsked about the tuna diet. "Madame, you will destroy their livers." I didn't yet understand the word for liver so wasn't sure what I was destroying and didn't heed their hardened advice.

It was the vets who got us on the drugs. "Madame, you may need this," the shorter one said as he rang up my triple-figure bill, sliding a box of Feliway across the counter.

"What is that?" I asked.

"It *calms* them."

We had to go to Normandy for a family thing, and Taups and Kraks were coming along for the weekend. I had grave fears the five-hour round trip would shred their nerves. So of course I added the 25-euro cat Valium to my tab.

We were soon hooked. We sprayed Feliway all over the apartment, as the little darlings had taken to clawing every vertical soft furnishing. MG used an industrial stapler to affix a strip of old carpet to the door for their use. They ignored it. Their favorite pastime was to claw circuits underneath our bed. The base looked like chicken chow mein.

On every weekend trip, they came with us. We would stop for a break and let them out of their boxes to roam, always for longer than anticipated as it's quite hard to dislodge a kitten from beneath a car seat. That may sound slightly stupid of us, but their non-stop meowing wore us down. The Radio FG compilations, as loud as they were, weren't enough to mask their wails. At pit stops, I'd bottle feed—just a bit of full-cream milk, to keep them happy and their fur shiny. I couldn't let them dehydrate, could I?

They tagged along on our summer holiday on a tiny island in Brittany—so tiny there are only six houses and you can only get there by boat, at certain points of the tide.

Out on the island, I fretted every night—had they come inside yet? What would happen if they didn't come in for the night? Alone, in the dark—anything could happen!

And then—your worst nightmare—one frisky twilight they both ran up a tree. I cajoled until my voice was a whimper. "C'mon, babies! C'mon! C'mon, babies! Taupo! Kraki! Come dooooowwwwnnnn!"

MG debated calling the fire station, but the tide wasn't at the right point, and besides, how could they bring their ladder? He climbed, of course, as high as he could into the dense cedar's blackness to rescue our babies from certain death. And we were certain they'd die up here; we could see Taupo was only going farther *up* the damned tree, not down. Oh, how I wanted to take a chainsaw to that trunk and end that horrible crisis.

This was all witnessed by MG's buddies since pre-school, who thought we were mad to be calling cats out of a tree way past *apéritif* time. It amused them to no end, the worrying about whether they were inside or outside. The freak-outs about the candles. "You know they're cats, right?" Manu pointed out.

"They're babies," I replied, cradling them close, ensuring that candles were extinguished upstairs and all remaining candles downstairs were huddled in one spot. What if one of them batted the naked flame? Paws on fire? Fur goes up *fast*. (There was no electricity on this island in Brittany, I might add. It was a seriously dangerous environment for infants.)

So, we survived that holiday with both Taups and Kraks intact. But only thanks to our vigilance. I was sure of that. MG and I were in perfect harmony on our parenting fervor. There was never a moment of, "The way I was raised, we'd definitely not be doing such-and-such." Or "My mom did it this way, so that's what we're doing for the girls." We didn't check in with each other or take a step back to see that we were both parenting cats as if they were children. (And inept, clumsy, delicate, gifted, hyper-sensitive children at that.)

The following summer, again, on the island, a new complication had arisen. I was expecting an actual baby.

We didn't know how to break this to the girls. They'd been communicating to me signs of an anxiety disorder. Or, should I say, anxiety disorder*s*, as surely their anxiety wasn't *identical*, they were both so unique and multi-faceted. We knew that because at one of our dinner parties—12-person affairs that lasted until four in the morning with booze and smoking out of windows—a scientist and wife pair had conducted some "experiments" with the cats in the bathroom and concluded that Krakatoa was more intelligent than Taupo. I didn't tell my friend, but this seriously offended me. Imagine if a guest took your children into another room to run intelligence tests on them and then told you their so-called results? Taupo was *just* as intelligent as her sister!

In any case, I was sure they had anxiety/anxieties. The Feliway just wasn't cutting it. MG had been in major do-it-yourself mode all that year: laying parquet, installing skirting boards, painting rooms, building a bookcase that stretched two meters by three, drilling in the overabundance of chandeliers and halogens that illuminated our every move. The cats had taken to knocking over their glass of mineral water on the feeding platform and harassing any new item that entered their space. Bouquets of flowers had to be put into something low, and plastic, after the glass tulip vase hit the floor. At night, lights off, they'd slip into our bedroom, and I'd have to scrunch my pillow down to accommodate them between the headboard and me.

I was worried about the impending birth of a human. Throwing that into the mix would be a live grenade. My mother had warned that cats sometimes creep into babies' cribs and suffocate them. I grew wary of our little girls, as if they could betray me at any moment.

On the island that summer, everything was... heavy. Me, the weather, MG attempting to read the booklet about which homeopathic treatments to give your wife as she labors (the only thing I read in preparation to becoming a parent). MG's friends sensed our complete non-preparedness and saw it as a good thing. Perhaps we were behaving normally for once. The late night drinking was a constant. But on the last night, I was beyond it—I was 35 weeks pregnant on an island with no easy escape when the tides were wrong, with no clue where the nearest hospital was anyway, and everyone downstairs was drunk and still drinking at 5 a.m.—and, dammit, the cats were *trying* to sleep but the noise was keeping them up!

We awoke early (me kicking MG to wake him) and cleaned the house meticulously before returning the keys to the owner. We wrestled the girls into their cages for the boat ride and six-hour hell-on-wheels of driving home to Paris. The cats were on banshee-mode and my body despised being strapped in a car seat so long.

We stopped to fill up on gas, where MG spent 20 minutes in the bathroom ridding his body of all the toxins from the previous night's drinking. I waited in the car at the pumps, the cats splintering their claws on the cage doors thinking a stopped car meant a bottle feed or perhaps a little run around. Nice. We were so ready for a baby.

Every time we left the apartment, our tortured darlings checked for escape routes. Devastated to be locked inside, again. I couldn't let them sit on the window box ledges. I'd read the news. A cat had *died* falling from a Parisian apartment window. We were on the third floor! With four-lane traffic streaming past our building on rue du 4 Septembre! MG hadn't had time yet to install the chicken wire netting on the ledge. And later, when he had, I still didn't like to let Taupo out on it. Birds might catch her eye, and she'd leap for sure.

So, human baby—born.

Came home from hospital.

Total and utter meltdown.

The cats sniffed the baby with suspicion as I held my breath. Would they accept their wee sister? Surely Kraks would take the lead and show some love?

Nope.

Krakatoa started peeing on the chesterfield.

Right in front of me, as I tried to get the hang of breastfeeding, at that stage when it's hell to get a good latch and your nipples feel like they've been set on fire, and your back aches, and you've only slept in 20-minute intervals since the birth, and your hooza needs a whoopee cushion because of the hemorrhoids.

That's when Kraki took to the couch, in a daily act of defiance, her green eyes glazing over as she stared me down and pissed.

That chesterfield had already been doused in Feliway

but they still clawed the heck out of it. We'd bought it, late one night after watching *24 Season 6*, off a Belgian vendor on eBay and upon arrival it reeked of cigarette smoke.

I tried cleaning the cat pee off the red leather, using state-of-the-art products from specialists, and then my niece's advice of orange, then pepper, but we had to admit this just wasn't working out.

We booked for large rubbish removal to take the thing away. I took about 100 photos of the chesterfield on the Paris sidewalk, looking like it had finally been given the chance to star in some avant-garde talk show.

Krakatoa continued to pull my insane-mommy trigger. She sneaked into the Stokke crib and slept in it. She rolled on clean baby laundry. She peed on parquet and even in the bathtub—shunning her deluxe cat shitter with those Italian f'ing air filters.

We had to call in help. MG's parents. They came and took her away. Our little ball of furry sweetness—and Taupo's daily shower—gone, gone on October 23, 2007. I remember her claws at the cage door, fervent and pathetic. I remember the cans of tuna I pressed into my mother-in-law's arms. I remember the look of pity at my tears.

But life continued. Taupo was remarkably brave about her loss. She never showed the typical signs of grief. She just started attacking any new person who turned up. Visitors bearing baby gifts got assailed. Nobody could lock the bathroom door without a white paw reaching in, claws extended. My octogenarian parents needed bandages and antiseptic wipes for the gouges. I heard Mom instruct through the walls: "Vic, stay away from that cat! You're on warfarin. She'll bleed you to death." Friends staying the weekend used earplugs to block the clawing-at-the-lounge-door all night.

Taupo went a few rounds with everyone. Suitcases were her specialty. My brother and his girlfriend came over from Canada, and eventually he pulled me aside. "Liz, I've never been scared of any cat, until now."

She woke up MG in a particular way every dawn: claw to groin area. Claw. To. Groin. It's a miracle MG remained viable to father another child. Of course, we weren't insane enough to allow *that* to carry on, so Taupo received the firm boundary of being locked in the lounge. I felt bad doing it but had no choice when faced with the lines of red on MG's upper thigh. Still, we could hear her hacking at the door late into every night. And every time the baby woke needing feeding, it set off Taupo. Claw. Claw. Claw. As baby fed back to sleep. I couldn't stop breastfeeding even though it still hurt like hell seven months post-birth because how could I enter the lounge/kitchen to make a bottle with Taupo there? I had to white-knuckle the night feeds and pray Béa would start sleeping through, and I could move her onto solids and be done with this nocturnal hell. That claw claw claw from the lounge wouldn't abate until I'd gotten baby back to sleep and crept into bed again, lying in silent wonderment that a cat could carry on *that long.*

One afternoon, I picked her up to move her so a cleaner could vacuum and in my shuffle to the door, in my woolen cardigan in the dry winter air, I gave the cat an electric shock. She leapt out of my arms, tearing a hole in my cardigan—and arm—with her back claws. *Far out,* that tuna made her claws strong and healthy. I crumpled to the floor, blood spouting from the six-inch gash. It looked like an attempt to kill myself. I wrapped my forearm in a dishcloth and rang MG at work. Actually *rang him at work*, it was that bad.

"What is it?"

"Taupo... my arm... scratch... I... I..."

"I'm in a meeting."

"I... it *hurts*."

"Call you later."

Click.

OK, no wonder I never called him at work. I canceled the afternoon's appointments and curled up on the corner of the couch.

So you can see where this was going. The militant vets stepped up their admonishments, almost staging an intervention. "Madame, the problem is Taupo is the *dominant,* and she sees your husband as the *subordinate.*"

"But she doesn't claw me, or the baby."

"She recognizes you are the top cat, but she is dominating your husband. She sees him as a lower cat."

"What can I do?"

I worried about how long I could keep Taupo—how long they'd let me keep her. I rang a cat psychologist. I don't even know where I found a cat shrink, but we only lasted one session. Marie-Estelle was way more interested in chatting up MG than in Taupo's troubled psyche. Her advice was to spray Feliway. Well, duh, we could've taken shares in the company! Sixty euros down the drain.

Things dragged on. The baby turned into a toddler. She crawled for nine months, probably to keep Taupo onside. You could watch Taupo's yellow eyes and read her mind: *If the small usurper stays on all fours then I remain the top cat.* Somehow our daughter knew this, and she and Taups got on great. There was only one incident where Béa crawled under a chair right up to Taupo's face... but the scratch wasn't deep—more a warning, really. It didn't scar her forehead. Unlike my "suicide attempt" slash or the numerous disfigurements MG bore.

We cohabited OK. Taups being locked in the lounge meant less room to accommodate guests, but then people stayed less and less anyway. When I was pregnant again, Taupo took to staring at me, unblinking, or lying beside my beach ball belly, purring madly. But I knew it had to end. In March 2011, Taupo joined Krakatoa in Normandy for *Papy dressage* (rehab Grandpa-style). The feeding platform looked bereft. With the deluxe cat shitter no longer needed, it became a glossy red kids' table with tea set, fake pastries, blobs of Play-Doh resembling cats. MG repaired the door. It took him two days and a whole tub of putty.

Taups and Kraks' rehab went incredibly well. Within a month, each transformed into a cat who slept in the garage, ate dry food only and killed a mouse if they needed something "wet." No clawing, no frenzy, no getting their heads stuck in a glass and smashing it to escape, no crisis up any tree, no falling out the window to certain death, no inadvertent fatal leaps.

The girls barely kissed us when we'd arrive for the weekend.

The only compromise was that Daniel, MG's dad, had to hack off half of the metal door handle in the garage because Kraki quickly learned to leap and pull down to open it. With only half a handle, she couldn't escape the garage. And so everybody slept, nobody's testicles were mauled, the cats reverted to, well, cats.

I guess being a normal cat wasn't enough for Taupo.

She and Kraki were staying at the cousins' house while MG's parents were on vacation. After a few days, the cousins didn't see any sign of Taupo in their garage—she had left by the cat flap. And never returned.

Was it altruism? Like some fated polar explorer wandering out into a blizzard to save the lives of others? No. It was spring. Nobody was dying of starvation and this was La Selle-la-Forge, not Antarctica. Did she fall in the stream and drown? Get stuck up a tree and perish? *Was* Taupo less intelligent than Kraks all this time and got herself lost in suburbia? My care and paranoia were for nothing?

I went house to house in search. In the days that followed, one woman saw the tip of a tail—an orange and white tabby tip—saunter past her kitchen window. That was our only sign.

Béa tells the story, of our cat who attacked everyone *but* her and Mummy. I came up with an ending with her that I think may be true: Taupo had had enough of cohabitation with Kraki—whom she had never entertained as anything more than a subservient push-around—and stalked the surrounds until she happened upon a little old lady with no other pets, who feeds her all the wet food she desires and lets her sleep anywhere she chooses and never has guests visit with suitcases and turns the tap on for her at will because *that's* what a top cat gets and that's who she is. Taupo *is*, not was. She is that caldera from the southern hemisphere's hugest eruption. She tolerated us imbeciles for far too long.

And... one day the dryer stopped working so MG dismantled it to repair. Curled up in the crawl hole behind the dial was that mouse, desiccated like an Egyptian mummy from the constant blast of hot air.

Forget Me Not
Stephanie Carroll

"You have to leave."

Myrtle had me hooked by the arm, escorting me to the front door.

"But you're my sister. They're my nieces—my nephew. I only have three days left."

She wrenched open the door and shoved me onto the front stoop. "No Lauraline, I only have three days left. Three days until this obsession and madness finally ends."

I squeezed my purse with both hands. "I just—"

She pointed back into her house. "Your nieces are terrified of you. William's crying. How could you tell them that?"

"They are older than we were."

She clenched her teeth, balled up her hands. "Clearly you don't recall what that was like." She jabbed a finger into her chest. "I was older. I saw what it did to you. To all of us."

I remembered my older sisters gasping and denying

it, calling Grandmamma Silvia a monster and a witch for telling an 8-year-old such a thing, especially so soon after our parents' deaths. "But someone had to tell them. I am old enough now to see the wisdom Grandmamma—"

"You are turning thirty, not ninety, and clearly you haven't an ounce of wisdom."

I looked down. "Will you still come?"

She crossed her arms and pursed her lips. "No. We won't be able to attend."

I grimaced.

"Don't worry. You'll see us again." She narrowed her eyes. "I will be sure to come by in not three, but four days."

I stood there on her stoop, pleading with my eyes, as if I were still eight. "But, I'll be dead."

She clenched her eyes shut and pointed out to the street. "Lauraline, just go. Please." She shook her head. "Damn Silvia for doing this to you." Then she slammed the door.

I rode two streetcars, then caught the train out of San Francisco back to Colma. About 40 minutes passed before I spotted the milky white of sculpted wings, carved pillars and rugged monoliths, obelisks, and rows and rows of tombstones. The fog had lifted and now hovered like a wool blanket in the sky. The moisture persuaded the grass and clover to turn exceptionally green this time of year, and it flourished among the dead. The train stopped at a few cemeteries before I exited at my station.

Colma is where San Francisco buries its dead. It's a little, unincorporated community just south of the city, close enough to visit by carriage, streetcar or train. There are 10 cemeteries already and talk of more ever since San Francisco passed that ordinance forbidding new burials within the city. All the dead come to us now. My grandfather was a sexton, and after he passed, my grandmamma said she had stayed in Colma to be closer to his whispers. She had asked if I could hear my father's whispers, but I never could.

I walked from the station, passing three cemeteries on the way to the house my grandmamma left me after she died. I had little other choice than to occupy it, despite my sisters' desire for me to move to the city. I wasn't exactly frugal with the little I earned taking down headstone engravings, so the house was of some use. Besides, I couldn't abandon the place where we grew up, a place that had so much of our grandmamma entwined within in its walls. They had avoided coming back to this place, but I insisted if they threw a party, they had to do it at the house. They'll forget Grandmamma when it's gone. They'll forget me too.

I stopped outside the iron-rod gate and stared at the house, recalling how it felt to lay eyes on it for the first time when I was eight. My parents must have avoided the house too because we did not see it until that dreadful day. To me, the house resembled a stack of decorative matchboxes stood on end, narrow and lofty as if it had wanted to rise above the clouds. A Belvedere tower loomed one level above the third story, and iron rods stuck up around the pointed roof. The doors and windows all stretched and thinned, and the wood carvings coiled and burst, manifesting puzzling ideas on the gabled pediments.

I looked over my shoulder, across the street to the edge of one of the graveyards, an area of which had been left vacant since I was a child. In the winter, the fog concealed the tombstones in the distance, and the grass and little purple forget-me-nots almost had a luminescence against the white. Just once, I told myself, just once I should go over there. But I knew I wouldn't. I had never set foot in that special place, not even as a child.

After my sisters called our grandmamma a witch, I spent a lot of time hiding in the labyrinth that was our new home. I slipped behind the secret doors in the paneling, played on the staircases inside the walls, and slunk around in the abandoned rooms. I used to skulk up the tower staircase into the attic and stare out the window, pretending that beyond the fog, the graveyard across the street was a meadow that went on forever. I used to imagine myself walking into the fog, disappearing into the endless white.

"What did you expect after telling the children that?" Carol-Anne lit the range with a match.

I plunked down and smashed my face between my hands. "How is it she can still make me feel like a child?"

Carol-Anne shrugged. "She's the oldest, the closest thing to our mother besides the Grand Silvia."

I laughed and sat up. "I completely forgot you used to call her that." Our grandmamma truly was grand. She was a wild and gaudy woman, which was why Myrtle took on a lot of the responsibility of raising us.

"Might I ask..." Carol-Anne grunted as she heaved a pot of water onto the range. "Why did you tell them?"

I took a deep breath, then let it out. "Grandmamma isn't around any more, so the responsibility to warn them falls to me. Myrtle certainly wouldn't tell them."

"Just to spite Grandmamma." Carol-Anne scooped up a mound of chopped onions, barley and peas, and carried them over to the pot.

"I thought... I don't know. I want them to remember me."

She tossed in some peeled potatoes. "Oh, I think they will remember you."

I groaned, covered my face and spoke through splayed fingers. "She's not coming to the party tomorrow."

"Well, we will be there, but please indulge me—don't tell Benny and Theresa any family stories."

"That was the last time I will ever see them. If they do remember me, it will be as the lunatic who told them if they have three children, the third girl is doomed to an untimely death."

"They won't. If the Grand Silvia was a loon, you'll have more time with them." Carol-Anne rubbed my back with her damp hand. "But if she wasn't, you'll be exonerated."

I looked up at her, amazed by her ability to make me feel better. How did my older sister become such an accomplished woman? Carol-Anne married a preacher, taught at a Methodist school for girls and spent her spare hours feeding the needy out of the church's dining hall. If anyone had an impact on this world, it was Carol-Anne. One merely had to spend an hour with her to witness her ability to turn any situation into that rare moment when a person's life can change. If only I could perform such a consequential act, then perhaps my life would have meaning, even if it was only in one person's opinion.

The kettle whistled.

Carol-Anne pursed her lips. "Didn't you come out to help?" She grabbed an apron and flung it at me.

I stood and slipped the apron over my head, tied it behind my back.

Carol-Anne lifted up a tray of graham biscuits and vanilla teacakes. "Fill the teapots and meet me out there."

I poured the steaming water into four mismatched porcelain pots, heaved up the tray and entered the dining hall where my sister had already delivered her treats. She was kneeling down to speak with a homeless girl. Blast.

Another one lost to Carol-Anne.

I scanned the room and spotted an old man, hunkered down, rubbing his hands together. It was a perfect opportunity. I'd pour him tea and say something that would change his life. I started in his direction, holding the tray high and my head too, when I felt a tug. I had stepped on one of my apron strings, and with my next step, my foot snagged the taut line. "Oh God." I hobbled, and the teapots slid to the right. "Damn! No!"

The clunky pots shattered at an old woman's feet, and scorching water splattered across her before completely spilling out and soaking her shoes. I covered my face with my hands and cringed as the tray clanged to the floor.

The woman leapt up, flapping and squawking like an angry chicken.

I reached out. "I'm sor—"

She recoiled. "Get away from me, you vulgar thing."

I stiffened, realizing that not only had I made a scene and worsened an already suffering woman's day, but I had also just shrieked several uncouth words in the church's soup kitchen. I looked around. Everyone glared at me as if I were Dickens himself. I turned toward Carol-Anne, whose upper lip had curled into an expression that demanded, *What on God's green earth is wrong with you?*

Five minutes later, Carol-Anne had wooed the woman back into graciousness, grabbed my coat and hat, and shuffled me out the back door. "At least you know the Lord, Lauraline. Count your blessings." She closed the door and clicked the lock.

I just want to be remembered when I die or at least feel confident that I did something meaningful in life. Clearly, it has come down to the last hour, and I want to have faith that I will fulfill a purpose, that I have one. You should know I do have faith in the Lord's design, even if I begrudge it a little.

I grimaced. "Don't write that part about begrudging it."

She scratched it out.

I took a breath.

The third girl in every Rosland family drops dead at the age of 30, the morning after the dreaded birthday, blood dripping from eyes, ears and nose. Tragically beautiful, is what Grandmamma used to say. Death only the day after one's youth has truly ended. This day seemed to come so fast, too fast to have prepared. What have I been doing for the last 30 years?

I stopped, pulled out my handkerchief, dabbed my eyes.

"Are you all right?" Sarah asked.

"I don't know what else to say," I said.

Sarah, the youngest of us four, wrote for a women's magazine, so naturally she had suggested I dictate my final words. I'm sure she had expected—even I had hoped—that in doing so I'd realize I had already made a difference. Unfortunately, that wasn't the case. To pile on the miseries, I had exhausted my time. The day was coming to a close. Tomorrow—the dreaded birthday. And then the day after that...

"I don't have anything to say that matters, no wisdom or life lessons to bestow, let alone anyone who will read this when I'm gone."

Sarah stuck the pen in its stand. "What about your nieces and nephews?"

"I don't want them to read this." I shook my head. "My life wasn't special. It was average and mediocre and eventless." I gestured toward the words on the Grand Silvia's yellowing stationery. "This won't last. Words and paper fade, new generations forget, lifetimes turn to smoke and drift away. Only those who have done something remarkable are held in others' memories. I don't even know why this matters to me so much. I'm just... I'm afraid." Her eyes met mine for a moment, and I had to look away because if I looked at Sarah, I wouldn't keep my wits about me. I gazed out the window at the people from the last train, ambling along, searching for the right cemetery before nightfall. Mourners always gawk at Grandmamma's house. It's such a curiosity and in such disrepair, I couldn't even donate it—another failed attempt to leave something behind.

"Don't think that way," Sarah finally said. "You shouldn't be sad these next two days. Remember good things, do something you love, be with family."

I twisted my handkerchief. "Myrtle's not coming."

She sighed. "I'll talk to her. She'll come."

I nodded but didn't expect her to persuade Myrtle. We sipped our tea, and I noticed the ticking of Grandmamma's assorted clocks.

Sarah set her hand on my knee. "I will stay with you... until..."

I forced myself to look at her, and when I did, my chin trembled and my body quaked. I couldn't do it any more. I folded over and wept into her lap. She *would* stay. She would stay until I collapsed and blood seeped through the lace of her dress, but I didn't want her to remember me that way.

Finally, I sat up and dabbed my eyes with my handkerchief, blew my nose and steeled myself again. "I want you to know." I sniffled. "I have accepted it. I have made my peace with God, and I am ready. I just don't want to be forgotten. That's all."

"You shouldn't worry so much about being forgotten."

I grasped her hand. "How would you feel?"

She lowered her eyes. "Lauraline, you can't—"

"I know," I said. "I know." I dropped her hand and looked back out the window.

The clocks ticked, and I heard Sarah's teacup clink on its saucer. She had given up and so had I. Outside, a gentleman craned his neck to peer in at us. We looked surprisingly young for such a rickety abode. Witches, presumably—young forever. I looked past him across the street at my eternal meadow and imagined disappearing.

After Carol-Anne, Sarah and I attended an emotional church service, we ate lunch and went to a vaudeville in the city. Then we rode the train to Colma. While it was still light out, Sarah collected flowers from the path by the gate, and Carol-Anne and I hung streamers in the dining room, squealing and laughing when the cobwebs caught in our hair. Our cooking efforts burst into an absolute mess in the kitchen, clumps of flour stuck in butter and chopped onions scattered across the floor. We hadn't cooked together since we were little, but we slipped right back into our girlhood ways. We teased and joked until Sarah and I made Carol-Anne fall to her knees in stitches. We had gotten into the currant wine by the time Sarah's husband knocked at the door.

When Carol-Anne's family arrived, Theresa and Benjamin, seven and nine, rushed over to me, excited to finally see my mysterious house.

"Do you want to go exploring?" I asked.

"Yes, yes!"

We slipped into the kitchen, passing Carol-Anne as she exited with drinks. "Not too long now," she called.

I revealed the hidden door next to the pantry, and we crept up the servant stairwell, and then escaped out the secret door behind the paneling in the second floor hallway. I whispered, "The last keeper of this house was a witch. Good or bad—no one knows."

"But *you* live here Aunt Lauraline."

"That must mean…" I bent down and widened my eyes. "I am the witch!"

They gasped dramatically and scurried away, giggling. We ran down the hallway and up the tower stairwell into the attic. Then we rifled through some of the dusty wardrobe trunks. I draped an old fur cape over my niece's shoulders and put my grandfather's faded derby on my nephew. I tucked an old autograph book from my 10th birthday under my arm. When we simmered down, I walked to the window that looked out over the graveyard in the gloom of day's end. I knelt down without minding the dust, and my niece plopped down in front of me. I wrapped my arms around her. "This was my favorite place when I was little," I said.

"It's so pretty," Theresa said.

"It's a graveyard," Benjamin said, unimpressed. "Dead people."

"Stop it Benny," Theresa said.

"But they are."

I touched his arm. "It was my place to be alone. This time of year, the fog rises in the morning, so it doesn't resemble a cemetery at all. I used to sit here and think it went on and on into forever."

"You played in a cemetery?"

"No." I shook my head. "I never went over there."

"Why?" Benjamin asked.

I sighed. "Because I didn't want to pretend. I wanted to walk into eternity and never come back."

My niece lay her cool cheek on my arm. "I'm glad you stayed, Aunt Lauraline."

I patted her shoulder. "Come along. Your mother is surely calling."

We raced down the narrow stairwell and into the front foyer where my niece and nephew spotted three blond children. They ran up to their cousins and begged permission to show them the house.

"Quickly then," Myrtle said.

I stared at Myrtle. "You came."

"Of course," she said with that motherly look in her eye. "I was angry before. I'm sorry."

I swallowed. "No, I'm sorry. I should never have—"

She embraced me so unexpectedly that I jumped. "Let's not speak of it," she said and then stepped back with my hands in hers. "This is a *happy* occasion." She nodded with big eyes, and I couldn't help but return a smile.

With that, Carol-Anne clapped her hands and announced dinner. The men heaved themselves up, and Carol-Anne called after the children. We moseyed into the dining room, and the children romped in chatting away about my house's secrets, which pleased me to no end. As we ate, my sisters and I monopolized the conversation: "Do you remember when Silvia insisted you wear that hideous fox?" "What about when I slipped on the ice and that dashing boy—oh what was his name?" "You hemmed it sideways, and I had to wear it or you'd cry." "Wait—you did what to that pudding? Lord, I ate it!"

For dessert, we enjoyed coffee and layered ribbon cake topped with pink buttercream icing. The children devoured their helpings and danced off into the parlor to play. Eventually they drifted to sleep and the husbands did too, but we sisters drank port and laughed until we exhausted ourselves. The rooms were prepared, so I insisted they stay. Myrtle and Carol-Anne nudged their families upstairs, but Sarah left her husband on the sofa, intent on staying with me.

Sarah and I fell into the Grand Silvia's plush loveseat, and I revealed the autograph book I had uncovered in the attic. By candlelight, we flipped through the pages, bemused by how we couldn't place the children from their names but could when we recalled a specific event or humorous attribute. We tried to think if we knew what had come of them. I pointed out how multiple children had written the same poems in the book, and which one I favored. We chatted between yawns until Sarah's head finally fell to the side. I fought the urge to kiss her cheek as I did the day she was born. Instead, I left the autograph book open to the poem we'd discussed.

I took a candlestick, crept upstairs and peeked in on Carol-Anne, squeezed into her childhood bed with Theresa. The men and the boys had taken Myrtle's old room, and Myrtle and her two girls slept in the Grand Silvia's room. I hovered in the doorway, certain my entrance would wake her. "You are a good sister and a good mother," I whispered. "Thank you for taking care of us."

I felt dizzy from the port but slipped behind the paneling into the secret passageway. Hunched down, I covered my mouth to keep from giggling with the memories of adventure I had in these walls. I exited into the kitchen and smiled at the foggy morning. I set the candlestick on the flour-coated table and blew out the flame. Then I pushed aside a headache and warm flush, and headed to the front door.

When I stepped outside, the chill stiffened me but felt fine upon my burning cheeks. The haze was so thick and the hour so early that it seemed as if no one existed at all. I went down the front steps, out the gate and across the street. I reached the edge of the graveyard, illuminated by the glow of the clover and the little purple forget-me-nots—my meadow. I stopped only for the briefest of moments before taking my first step into the sacred space. The grass crunched, frozen beneath my feet. Soon the morning frost would melt into a dew, making a cool bed for me to lie upon. I stood there for a moment, considering this first step, a simple act that I had been dreaming of since childhood. I took a deep breath and began to walk, steady, confident.

The time had finally come. I had wondered how I would feel, yet, right at that instant, I couldn't say. The intensity of the moment numbed my heart as the cold numbed my fingers and toes, but my mind raced. I had spent my last days trying to matter but had failed to accomplish anything of significance. What did that mean? Had I made peace with the fact that I would inevitably fade from memory as if I had never existed at all? Or in the wake of this moment, does it just not matter? What of my life then? Had I lived? My family—was I content with the way I left them? Our disagreements had dissolved into laughter—but was it enough? Was anything I had done enough?

White surrounded me for some time until little shapes appeared in the distance, and I knew I was close to the other side. I stopped and looked back at the house towering above the fog. I envisioned my sleeping family inside and pictured them waking, stretching, yawning. I thought of Sarah sitting up on the Grand Silvia's loveseat and looking around for me, only to find the autograph book opened to the poem. I hoped she would read it to them. They were not my words. They were not the words of those children. We could not take credit for the verse's significance, and yet it elegantly stated what we truly wanted to say all along. I wasn't alone in that sense, which in itself was comforting.

An aroma like my grandmamma's gingersnaps wafted in the air, and I could almost make out a tune, a whisper—my father whispering a song my mother used to play on her piano. I could hear his whispers, and I remembered that they used to sing. I had lost that memory along the way. What else had I lost?

I winced as pain pierced through my thoughts. I

pressed the back of my hand to my forehead, radiating heat. A tickle drew my fingers to my lip, and I pulled back to see a drop of blood lingering on my finger.

I took a deep breath, lowered my hand and took in one last glimpse of my grandmamma's house—my house. I turned away, away from my house, away from my family, and I walked. I walked into the white, into my eternal meadow and disappeared.

There is a small and simple flower,
That twines around the humblest cot,
And in the sad and lonely hours,
It whispers low: "Forget me not."

-A common verse found in autograph albums at the turn of the century

Bound by Water
Maureen Foley

"We come and go, but the land is always here. And the people who love it and understand it are the people who own it—for a little while."
-Willa Cather, *O Pioneers!*

On our Hass avocado ranch, the sky turns dark and my daughter sleeps at the opposite end of our sage green house. I am her air, she breathes, too much pressure. Nostalgia, her upcoming third birthday, and the late afternoon ground fog crawl the land and linger before clearing now, leaving only a faint sadness. The sky becomes night-gray. I am learning to be a sixth-generation California farmer, from my family, from the land, from the accidental death of the two new avocado trees I planted last year that didn't quite make it. Someday, I will give my baby girl all of our family's avocado, blood orange, Blenheim apricot and pomegranate trees, along with the boysenberry brambles, hibiscus, Cecile Brunner roses, scented geraniums, rosemary. All of it, every plant named and anonymous, hers.

But first, I want to give her the story of her birth. I will hold her hand to my stomach and show her the cleaved flesh, the light pink and shiny scar like a row of earth rototilled by a man's hand, surgeon's knife blade, where the doctor reached a hand in and took her. Too young now, she sleeps in the early evening as I step through the torn screen backdoor to walk the land and think of the day she made me hers. Just before darkness now. Two red-tailed hawks fly over, and I feel an overwhelming wingbeat of apprehension, an elusive unease ever-present since the moment my daughter arrived.

Forget that. She never arrived. She split me open.

Now having her alive in the world, I risk losing so much more. The land continues on without us, cyclical droughts and floods and fires and insects that sting or don't and never needed any of us. I walk down the three cement steps, away from my house, into the patch of Albion strawberries, where I sunk 75 bare root plants last year. Beyond the weedy rows of fruit and skinny blueberry bushes and wilted rhubarb plants, hundreds of Hass avocado trees span out in neat rows, 10 feet apart, corded at their ankles by irrigation sprinklers.

We are bound by water here in Southern California, tree to tree, rancher to crop. This year my father showed me how to "do the water." For the first time, he explained how the sections of our family's ranch are divided by irrigation valves, how lack of water pressure means that the groups of trees must be watered in shifts. The entire parcel takes 10 days, during the summer, to receive its dose, its cure, its feeding of di-hydro oxygen. We pay for the water we use, and this geography is actually coastal desert. My family is the current temporary caretaker here, in this land inhabited for thousands of years by Chumash peoples, hunting, fishing, eating acorns—like the ones littering my driveway with thousands of castoff seeds. Nothing original, no new thoughts. My daughter and I just repeat the breath of those before us. I wonder how soon the water here will run dry.

When or how my baby's placental water broke is confusing. Nearly 24 hours before my daughter was born, I woke up damp in my own wet bed. Did I pee in the night? Was it the first sign of labor? I'd read so many books and websites about the predictable patterns of birth, that, by that point, I was shocked by the mysterious vagueness of my own labor. My body gave away nothing: no clues, no clear baby pain, no sensation whatsoever. Just the mortification of sleeping in and on my own bodily fluids, not sure what to make of it. Was that really mine? Urine swimming or something else? Water, membranes broken, passive voice, something done to the pregnant mother—me—but by who? My love, I give her credit. The baby busted me down, and that strange, thin water-that-is-not-water gathered around the broken shipwreck of my creaking form. Underneath the physical sensation stirred the patter of concern: Was my baby still alive and well, now that her bathtub home collapsed inside me? I couldn't feel a child moving any more. Would the baby make it safely into the world?

No matter. Tears now flow. I receive them. I cry, but I try to make no sound because there's no real reason for this flood on my face. Every baby is born of pain, a woman's curse, we're told, and children replace us and a woman's lot is misery. A Buddhist's path is one of suffering, pain, but not like this. Three years later, I'm still walking one foot after the other on the ranch, so much slower at the moment because of the recent rain's overgrowth, through knee-high malva weeds and yellow-bloomed sour grass. Take a left, past the corner of the house, feet crushing dead MacArthur avocado leaves, through tangled, round nasturtium greens and blossoms, past one lit bedroom window and one dark bedroom window where my daughter sleeps. Quietly, I unlatch the waist-high wooden gate into my front yard just as an orchard rat scuttles up the avocado tree behind me, and I flinch.

A mother is born with her baby. I wanted a natural earthbound birth and the chance to collect my daughter's placenta, to dry and eat it, to bury some of her birth shroud under an avocado tree on the ranch to guarantee her natal pull back to this land. But instead my water broke mysteriously in the night, after I'd taken a Vicodin to calm the strange pain in my hip that capsized my body to a reclined position and left my leg useless, paralyzed. I fell down the birth rabbit hole of medical interventions, exactly the things I'd fought against: epidural for the hip pain, then Pitocin to speed the labor, then full dilation, pushing, the anesthetic ran out, panic, breathing, chanting, droning, a fever rising, infection and a growing panic that led to a come-to-Jesus moment with my husband. The obstetrician demanded a Caesarean, and I fought him at first. I wanted to push some more, until my husband stared me down.

"Mo, we're having a C-section," he implored, inches from my face, as if both our bodies were being severed and knifed and slit. I nearly puked from the overripe smell of my husband's coffee breath, the terror of my worst nightmare becoming flesh.

"Just leave me alone, for a second," I begged. "Please?" Nurses, doctor, husband. Everyone left the room.

Hand curled around a small metal Thai Buddha statue, I cried and cried because of course I wanted to see my baby as soon as possible—but not by force. I was failing as a mother already, a new statistic in the War

Against C-Sections. All of my natural birth class teacher's advice about the dangers and complications of having a C-section—for mother and baby—tormented me. In that moment of pure reptilian fear, I wanted to die rather than face surgery. One breath, and the urge to hold my first and only child surfaced and blotted out the terror.

When my husband walked back in the darkened labor and delivery room about two minutes later, I agreed to the surgery. And within 20 minutes, they'd segmented my guts, heaved them aside, and found a 10-pound, nine ounce girl inside a marshy bog of my infected birth fluids. There, in the hospital operating room, the surgeon immediately declared my afterbirth a biohazard, infected, like my daughter and me. A mystery virus, a sickness that drove up my fever, made my baby's first appearance in the world covered in the green foul meconium filth of newborns, sent her to the Neonatal Intensive Care Unit, and made my already hellish post-partum recovery even thicker with degrees of unease. How I first held my daughter—not when she was born, but later, the next day, in the NICU. We were surrounded by heartbroken parents whose babies were marooned like prisoners in isolettes with tubes and monitors, waiting for the right doctors to OK the right milestones so we could all take our babies home. Finally, home at last.

But before that, just after the C-section, the doctor filled my veins with the morphine derivative fentanyl, and I left my body. I surrendered the heartbreak of abandoning my newborn to well-trained strangers without being able to hold her. I was lost to a deep, drugged-out Hades realm of the unconscious. This made me temporarily postpone any feelings of regret, fear, miserable gloomy anxiety that something serious plagued my new baby, all gone for a few hours, only to become my constant shadow for days and years later, like an aftershock, still felt keenly with each of my daughter's birthdays. What if? What if something should happen to her? What if her flawed birth has cursed her to larger problems down the line?

My daughter and I fled the hospital six days after her birth and returned to the ranch, and there's a photograph from her first day at home that I find irresistible. Puffy from the surgery and pregnancy, my round face is framed by hundreds of almond-shaped avocado leaves, in varying shades of yellow-green. I'm wearing a white, button-up maternity blouse, for easy access to breastfeeding. It's loose to keep any fabric from my fleshy wound, the thin-lined, red five-inch incision just fingertips above my pubic bone. I'm holding my daughter on her land, like the timeless mother of forever, and there is no way not to be in love with everything about this image. My face holds the infinite weight of terror and pride I'm feeling, knowing I've just signed myself up for a lifetime of devotion and worry.

"We've made it home, to the dirt," my face says. "To where we're safe, for now."

On the ranch, I'm walking by the road near our house, Highway 154, where during the brief periods between the cutting down of one orchard of avocados and the planting and maturing of a new one, a sliver of the Pacific Ocean is visible. Trees hide that gem from view now. Instead, I can see the lit bedroom windows of the little green house, like eyes, glimmering at me kindly in the dark. I could keep walking away, away, down this winding asphalt byway. I want to stroll all night and not look back.

I could escape the relentless anchor of this geography, my family, the sadness of relatives and dreams and time gone to sleepless nights of my daughter's coughs and wet diapers and money woes and lost jobs. I could, but there is no place except here and no one for me, except my husband, the writer, crouched like a hunting white egret perched still over laptop-marshland, in his office. I could, except my baby girl sleeps, and she needs me, wants me to tell her stories, read her books. And no one knows her like her mother. I'm her mother, dear mother. From a desire to flee, my heart now feels the pull back to her. Like a drug, I am compulsively drawn to peek in on her in the night, that demanding toddler turned still by sleep. Who will give her the real birth story, the truest tale of what it was like to make her and birth her and find her beached onto the shores of her air-trapped new life?

I jog back toward home, cold, between the rows of Hass avocados, careful not to trip in a gopher hole. I can't see much in the dark, but there's relief in facts. Term pregnancy, delivered. Early post-partum hemorrhage, chorioamnionitis. Today, I re-read my own medical records. I can hear Dr. Vega's steady, firm voice transcribing his notes now: "A low-segment transverse incision was made in the uterus with a scalpel and extended both ways using bandage scissors... The baby was delivered onto the field... It was a female infant... The skin was approximated with staples... At the end of the procedure, the needle count, instrument count and sponge count were correct." It's shocking to see myself through the eyes of a surgeon, as a project, a victim, a hunk of anesthetized human meat. The language is as sterile as his instruments, his touch is as cold and distant as his emotions, and my body is just an obstacle to the true goal: the healthy baby sealed within my fleshy package. The objectification of my carcass is complete, more than any catcall or sexist remark or look a man can give that says I'm his. I'm nothing but a means to his end. The frigid dismemberment of my female form is complete and wholly disturbing. There is no life left in his words. Not like on the ranch, where every square inch vibrates with organisms. Here, I will build her a tree house, at home, in our orchard, and she can pick whichever tree she wants. I'm back at the front door of my daughter's sleeping house, and I blink at the cloud of flies and moths pounding the outdoor lamp, threaded over with cobwebs.

This is hers now, all I see, know, think. Soon, we'll celebrate that third birthday with all-pink everything. I am gone to her, and I will give her my body, my slender scar, my stretch-marked stomach and hours lost to no sleep and no work and no writing and no art nothing because I needed to know her, to know her breath, to rustle her air and become her heartbeat and then to watch her become delivered of this place, her land, my ranch. Ten pounds of baby now 30-some pounds of little girl. I walk inside the quiet house, and the land ignores me again forever. An avocado falls, a mother is born, a child keeps sleeping, and rows of dancing avocado leaves still the night, goodnight.

Two Kinds of Legacy
Jenny Milchman

This is what happened to me one day in sixth grade.

I went to school, expecting it to be pretty much like any other day. I would struggle to keep up with math and geography. (I didn't know then—a lot of people didn't know back then—that there were such things as learning disabilities and for me this meant that spatial things were hard.) I would enjoy language arts, but get scolded for chit-chatting with friends by my teacher, who called me Motor Mouth. (Were teachers meaner then? It seems like it.) At lunch my friends and I would play Chinese jacks or maybe have a food fight or practice our latest dance number. We were drama kings and queens.

The aforementioned friends were quiet during the morning, so I didn't get in trouble for talking in language arts that day after all. But I didn't have any real inkling what was going on until I headed to lunch.

Many of you probably recall those tables with the bench seats attached. The table where you sat was decided by which clique you were in. And the particular placement of your seat on the bench was decided by which position you held in the clique.

If sixth-graders ruled the world, it would be a feudal lordship.

I entered the lunchroom with the slightest tug in my stomach, which I knew wasn't from hunger. My friends were acting weird. And kids can usually tell when something is up; sometimes it just takes a little while to face it.

I crossed the gleaming white floor—the food fights hadn't started yet—and headed toward my table.

My usual seat was on the bench facing the entrance. Smack in the middle of the bench because I held a pretty choice spot in my group. We weren't the most popular, sporty kids in school, but we had our own sanctified place as the drama bunch. And since my best friend, Karen, was the director of our all-kid acting troupe, I guess you could call me next-in-line to the queen.

Everyone was seated already, and it was clear my spot was no longer reserved for me. Instead there was a line of hard, implacable faces. Just in case I hadn't figured it out, my friends all inched a bit closer as I drew near, filling in any available cracks of space until I was met with a solid wall of rejection.

Not a word was exchanged; understanding was as silent as it was instantaneous. I wheeled around, and before a teacher, lunch lady or any other adult could spot me, I exited the lunch room. I marched down the hall, head held high but feeling like a hundred pound weight. My stomach was completely done for; it didn't matter that I was cutting my lunch period for there would be no eating that day.

I waited until I turned the corner to lean against a wall so I could try and catch my breath.

Where is there for a turned out sixth-grader to go? In class I could hide amidst my work, pretend I didn't notice or care that no one was talking to me, and that I would never be known as Motor Mouth in that school again. But lunch was unsupervised time for children, *Lord of the Flies* time. My space had been quietly swallowed up as if I were no more. It was like I didn't exist.

There was only one place in school whose inhabitants didn't care if you were friendless.

The library.

Of course, I wasn't supposed to be in the library during lunch. The prescribed times to check out books were more codified than our seats on the lunchroom benches, but arguably less rigid. I slipped through the door and sidled over to a shelf of books. I sank to the floor, and then, surrounded by friends truer than those who were spurning me, I began to cry.

The librarian must've become aware that her quiet, lunchtime-empty space was no longer unoccupied. She was an obese, warty woman who could've been a character from a book herself: a gnome or a troll. Yet that day, and for every day during the remainder of that long, lonely year, she looked like the Blue Fairy in *Pinocchio* to me.

When Ms. Schultz spotted me on the carpet amidst a tumble of welcoming books, she didn't catch my eye. She averted her head and shuffled on by. She never said hello or asked if I needed help finding something. If she didn't acknowledge I was there, then she could just leave me be, in one place that still wanted me.

What legacy will we leave behind, all of us? Will we be the child who turns on another kid and ruins a year of her life, or leaves her with memories so bitter, they can make her cry more than 30 years later? Will we be a librarian nobody thinks much of, but who turns out to be the true heroine of this tale?

Our legacy is cast back when we are far too young to understand such a concept, to know that such a thing even exists.

I came to school the following day, and nothing had changed. My so-called friends spoke not a word to me during class; a space was no longer reserved for me at lunch. I sometimes wonder, with the hindsight of adulthood, what would have happened if I had tried to sit down. The judgment wielded by sixth-graders is firmer than that of any high court judge. If everyone could obey the way we did when part of a group of middle-schoolers, law and order would rule the land.

For me there was no appeal, no seeking of a governor's pardon. I accepted my sentence without even understanding the crime I'd been convicted of. I still don't understand it. But I understand its legacy.

When I began researching this piece, I delved into online accounts of girl meanness, as well as more in-depth works of social psychology. The internet would have that one source of girl-on-girl cruelty is insecurity. By putting another girl down, especially publicly, the first girl secures a place for herself, and the illusion that she must be better, thus bolstering her own fragile, adolescent sense of self.

There is also a relational perspective to girl meanness, which says girls break the world down into associations and connections, and that deciding whom to revere, whom to tolerate and whom to ostracize is all part of spinning an understandable web of which person belongs where.

I have a daughter now, and I am constantly trying to impress upon her that the offhand comment she or a friend may fling can leave a lasting legacy on the person who hears it. It's a large burden for my daughter to carry, I know. Not only does she have to navigate the surging seas of elementary school—apparently girl meanness starts younger these days—but her mother is imploring her to consider that the direction she swims in could have an effect years and decades later.

It's too much for a child. And yet how can I screen out the awareness that my daughter is imprinting her legacy on lives with every friend she makes, every joke she laughs at, every anecdote she tells?

In many ways, I was particularly vulnerable to this kind of meanness as a child. Whereas both of my own children laugh off any comments that come their way, I took every single one to heart.

I was a scared child. Other kids could have great fun at my expense because I was so gullible. I remember a boy at a play date—though we had a different name for kids getting together then, or rather, no name for it at all—telling me that the fresh-out-of-a-package chocolate cookies his mother had served were poisoned. I spent the remainder of the time at his house sure I was going to die.

And yet this child likely had no idea of the impact his words would have. That he was leaving a legacy. So many of the things we do and experience as children leave marks, even though we live in a transitory, impermanent way then, as if our actions were sand on a beach, repeatedly washed away by the next wave.

My sixth grade woes didn't go away. I spent each day hiding from the fact that I no longer had friends. Another aspect of girl meanness is the sense of shame some feel, while others are able to laugh off what happens or get angry about it. The ones who feel ashamed, who take in what is being done to them as if it is their fault, tend to keep on being victims. And that is what happened to me during many of my subsequent school years.

Pushed into outsider status, I grew used to the position. I can't say I ever embraced it—I have memories of walking into the girls room in high school and wishing everyone luck as they suited up for that day's lacrosse game, knowing that wasn't the right thing to say, yet still being crushed over the giggles I heard as I walked out—but I did begin to get something from it. An ability to watch and listen and learn.

Flash forward to adulthood. We do grow up and leave school behind forever, even if that's hard to believe at the time. I had a dream of being a writer, although it's a chicken/egg quandary whether my love of reading drove my desire to write, or the fact that I was going to become a writer triggered my love of reading. Either way, one of the few things that did garner me popularity as a child was when I was asked to tell a story aloud to my friends or write a scene for one of our plays.

But by college graduation, I was still almost completely unformed as a writer. The peripatetic wanderings of my pen relied on a handful of core preoccupations that have persisted to this day—mostly having to do with nature—but couldn't stand up to the rigors of structure or medium or genre. I wrote about whatever was going on in my life. There are some writers who can make a career of such inward examination, but I wrote in circles with no clear sense of craft.

A more concrete career path presented itself in the form of psychotherapy, and after pursuing a graduate degree, I went to work in a rural community mental health outpost. I had never been more outside of things: I was a fly on the wall of my clients' lives, the stranger who heard about their intimate relationships without ever playing a part. But my job also helped me see that everyone feels small and unlikeable, helpless and atrocious at times. No one is an insider always.

One day, a mother brought her little girl in to see me.

The child was a blond-haired, 5-year-old cherub who had just killed the family pet.

In an instant, my life went from fairly normal to a stream of events that were like something out of a suspense novel. And just as I'd found respite in stories all those years ago in sixth grade, so did the same thing happen now. My day-to-day had become overwhelming—I was responsible for figuring out what was wrong with people in truly dire circumstances. For solace and consolation, I began reading suspense and mysteries. One day, I ceased the aimless wanderings of my pen, and sat down at a keyboard and began to type.

Much as the duckling turned into a swan, the gullibility that plagued me as a child suddenly became a benefit: It was a conduit to chilling tales. Being an outsider was also no longer a liability; it allowed me to bring characters to life, studying their traits and foibles and conflicts so I could turn them into real, fleshed-out human beings on the page.

During this time when I was realizing the tales I was always meant to pen were thrillers, stories of women facing demons inner and outer, I continued to practice as a psychotherapist.

One day, a mean girl came into my office.

She had a polished sheet of hair and gleaming blue eyes. She was depressed and needed help, and I was a paid mental health professional, not a sixth-grader, so I set aside my associations to the girls who had ostracized me, and began therapy instead. This girl revealed the countless careless cruelties she inflicted on kids less pretty and popular than she. But she also shared how unloved she felt at home compared to her little sister. The ire she turned on other kids was a translation of what she received from her father and stepmother.

As our work together progressed, I got an inkling of how even the meanest of girls harbor deep fears and insecurities and feelings of self-loathing. Suddenly, far from being an outsider, I was as inside as it was possible to go. Deep in the inner recesses of a mean girl's motivations and mind.

My patient's legacy turned out to be far worse than girl meanness, however.

Late one night, I was called to the ER where my patient had been brought following a car accident. She wasn't terribly injured, although she hadn't regained consciousness yet. When she did, she was going to learn that her little sister, who had been with her in the car, had not survived the accident.

Legacy comes in two forms: that which we leave behind, and that which leaves an impact on us. How was my patient going to live with hers?

During the next 10 years, as my psychotherapy career gave way to an increasing drive and urgency to become a published author, one preoccupation in my stories became clear. I was writing about the meanness life harbors. About criminals and conspiracy, snatchings and searches, intruders and invasions.

But beneath these surface dangers, I was writing about the fate of the outsider. My heroines were all outsiders in their own lives.

Nora Hamilton, in *Cover of Snow*, has come to the small, fictional town of Wedeskyull as the wife of a local policeman. When he dies unexpectedly and violently, she will have to breach the walls of this unwelcoming place to find answers.

Liz Daniels, in *Ruin Falls*, is local to Wedeskyull, but she's a stranger to her own marriage and to the husband she thinks she knows. That the most intimate of allies can turn us into outsiders in our own lives is the lesson Liz will have to learn.

And in *As Night Falls*, Sandy Tremont is a stranger to herself. She has kept hidden the source of her deepest pain, and in the secrecy lie the seeds of her undoing.

I was an outsider for a long time, and whenever I sit down to champion another woman's journey, from someone who is a stranger in one way or another to someone who ultimately learns about herself, I become a bit more of an insider. In the lives of my characters and also within myself.

One bookseller to whom I owe thanks—and there are many—said that when she finishes reading one of my novels, she feels stronger.

And don't we all need to feel that way? In my truest, most peeled away bare moments, I am still that sixth grade girl, finding solace in a shelf of books.

But I am someone else now, too. A writer who gets to lose herself in tales. A mother and wife and friend with the wisdom garnered from 10 years of treating people in need.

Sometimes I see another girl, caught in the throes of pain it will take her decades to understand. Or a mean girl, unaware of the pain she inflicts and that which may still come her way. My patient or someone like her.

She enters a room full of books. She picks one up, and finds both respite and rescue in the story.

The book she is reading is mine.

It's my legacy.

A Forever Home
Regina Calcaterra

"My name is Brezan, I am twenty-one, and I want a family."
Finding a street spot to park my car on the Upper West Side of New York is never an easy task—especially on a Sunday near the historic Riverside Church. To my surprise, I found a space just big enough to fit my Prius a mere block away. This was fortunate since I was already late to You Gotta Believe's first faith-based meeting with church leaders and congregation members.

Ten years ago, I read an article in *The New York Times* about You Gotta Believe, an organization that works to get older foster children adopted. While I was a teenager in foster care in the 1980s, I was told that when I "aged out" of foster care on my 18th birthday, I could expect to be homeless. (The "age out" age varies from state to state.)

Back then, when I asked my case worker if I could be adopted instead of being homeless, she told me foster kids are not adoptable, especially the older ones. The weight of her words reinforced what others had told me:

The clock was ticking, and my options for a decent life were narrowing. At age 38, after reading about You Gotta Believe and its mission of finding permanency for our foster youth, I had immediately contacted the organization's founder and offered my assistance. I have been serving on its board of directors ever since.

As a foster care child, I personally experienced the shortcomings of the government system and its challenges serving as a pseudo-parent to foster children. After joining You Gotta Believe, I was elated that an organization outside of the government infrastructure existed to identify and train prospective foster-adoptive parents and that it believed that regardless of age, every child deserves a forever home.

I jumped out of my car and raced toward the church, but halted in confusion when I looked up. The church takes up more than a city block with one entrance after another (after another). It was huge and intimidating, but I picked a door and rushed inside the large sanctuary.

As an advocate for adoption of foster children, I've been active in speaking and writing on the issue. As a foster child, I lived through these issues. But taking the message inside one of the most hallowed houses of God in New York had never crossed my mind. That is, until one weekend several weeks earlier. While speaking at a foster care adoption awareness weekend at Arizona's Sun Valley Community Church, I heard a state executive publicly pronounce that government cannot be a good parent. Of course, as a child of the system, I could agree. But if not government, then whom? Or what? Faith-based institutions?

Inside Riverside Church, I didn't see pews but found a polite security officer, who directed me to a room on the fourth floor. I quietly opened the door and slid unnoticed into the back row.

The room's five long rows of chairs were filled with a

cultural and generational mix of congregants. Up front was a tall and broad gentleman who appeared to be the leader, sitting at a desk facing the congregation and nodding at key points raised by the speaker. He would then look at the crowd, and smile and nod again as if in approbation of the speaker's premise. Mary Keane of You Gotta Believe stood confidently without a podium before the congregants. Mary has become a forever parent to 13 young adult women from foster care and trains prospective parents on how to be forever or adoptive parents to older foster children.

Mary explained that annually, more than 20,000 children in the United States age out of foster care and end up alone—with no parents or family to guide them during the difficult transition into adulthood. No one to be present in their adult lives. These young men and women will be pushed out of foster care and into society without a safety net to rely on when any setback occurs, and many will end up homeless, incarcerated or worse.

Mary reminded the congregation how these children landed in foster care. "They are not bad children; they were just dealt bad hands." She paused to gauge the response in the room, as not only the leader nodded in acceptance but the church members as well. She let that sink in, before she told us what actually happens to our foster children when they age out, parentless. "Part of the problem is that before aging out of the system, older foster children are provided lessons on how to live independently rather than what they really need—a parent," she told us. "Instead of holding our breath and crossing our fingers hoping that the independent living training will work for them as we kick them to the curb, we need to change course and find them forever homes."

The lineup of speakers that evening included three kids I knew from my work with You Gotta Believe. Then there was a fourth.

Susan Grundberg, the executive director of You Gotta Believe, turned to catch my gaze and mouthed, "Just listen." And then she pointed to me and said, "You will like her." She was right.

I looked back at the young woman who stood before us in a black and white jersey dress with horizontal stripes and practical black ballet flats, totally at ease and exuding a sense of "I got this" to the audience. She was Speaker Number Four.

"My name is Brezan, I am twenty-one, and I want a family."

Brezan told the audience she had been placed in foster care at age 16 after her school found out that her father, with whom she lived alone, was abusing her. She awoke that morning, went to school, was corralled by counselors, and that afternoon was carted away to a foster home, never to see her father again. She remained in foster care and was taught the usual independent living skills to prepare for living on her own when she aged out of care. However, she was convinced that college was a better path to independence. As the congregants sat in silence, clinging to her words, Brezan explained how she was putting herself through a private college and was only one semester away from graduating. She shared that although she had done this all on her own, she still wanted a parent, so she could have one for the rest of her life. We all nodded in understanding, nodding in unison. Don't we all want a parent for the rest of our lives, that safe place to always go back to? Someone to share holidays and birthdays with? Someone to call when something momentous—good or bad—happens?

Her case worker never told her that she could be adopted and that she deserved a forever family. It was only through her therapist that she learned she could have parents. This therapist had sought to become a certified foster-adoptive parent of a foster youth, beginning the process by taking state-mandated training classes. She happened to take these classes at You Gotta Believe and learned that older foster children are adoptable. She learned that in fact it is never too late for a family. It is never too late to find someone to love you.

She immediately told Brezan about You Gotta Believe, just one month before Brezan would turn 21 and get kicked out of the system. Brezan called You Gotta Believe, and within a few weeks appeared on Wednesday's Child, a weekly televised program that features foster children who are waiting to be adopted.

Susan must have sensed my excitement in hearing Brezan, so when she turned to me, I asked why she was keeping Brezan from me. She smiled and said, "You know, she is the closest thing to your mini-me I have ever met." She was right; I saw myself in the fearless but vulnerable girl at the front of the room.

After the event's conclusion, throngs of congregants surrounded Brezan. She may not have realized it, but her courage and dramatic presentation shifted the views of many in the room. She totally won them over.

I had planned on driving home right after the event, but instead stayed, in line, waiting for all of Brezan's new fans to exhaust their enthusiasm so I could get a moment with her. After a full hour, I realized that the only opportunity for quality time with this amazing pillar of strength was to offer to drive her home to Brooklyn, an offer she instantly seized. It beat trying to make subway and bus connections operating on a weekend schedule.

While walking to my car, I told her I was affiliated with You Gotta Believe and had aged out of foster care myself while in college back in 1987, the same way that she did 27 years later in 2014—parentless with no adult connections or resources.

As we drove down the West Side Highway to the Battery Park Tunnel to Brooklyn, I told Brezan that I recently published a memoir about how my siblings and I grew up scraping for food, bouncing in and out of the foster care system. Brezan, curious about the book, looked it up online on her phone. She immediately recognized the book cover and told me her therapist had read it and had asked her to read it too, but Brezan said she felt it too difficult to read at the time.

The rest of the drive back to Brooklyn we shared our respective stories and compared all of our similarities. After Brezan appeared on Wednesday's Child, she was introduced to a family in New Hampshire that expressed interest in adopting her. She was days away from finally meeting them.

They had bought her a bus ticket up to New Hampshire on Christmas Eve. Since I knew she would have a long bus ride, I offered her a copy of my memoir to read on the way.

After Brezan returned from an enjoyable week with her prospective new family, I extended her an invitation to spend a weekend with me at my house on Long Island.

Contrary to most college students, who could enjoy the breaks between semesters with family, Brezan had to work. Her schedule as a home health aide limited her free time during the few weeks before the fall and spring college semesters. That was yet another reminder that as a child without parents, she had only herself to depend on to keep her head above water. Eventually, she found time to visit me, where she bonded with my cocker spaniels and enjoyed a tour of the North Fork's beaches, farmland and wineries.

Throughout our brief 30-hour visit, I had to keep reminding myself that this confident young woman, who appeared ready to conquer the world, was actually parentless and potentially one step away from homelessness. Where others not familiar with her background would infer that her self-determination, tenacity and optimism were enough to propel her forward, I knew better. We all need a safe to place to put our heads down and adults we can count on when that ominous dark cloud tries to sneak into our lives.

Our visit ended, and I dropped her off at the rail station. I told her I wanted to be a resource for her. In foster care, when children age out, they are at risk because they are left alone at such a young age, and yet we expect them to survive. We need to get them forever homes or at the very least become a resource to them. A resource is an adult who supports them and will be available when needed. If aged-out youths have a community of resources (group of adults), they will have a safety net to help them move forward and catch them when they fall. Resources can either take the place of or supplement the adoptive parents, because the goal is to build a safe community of adults around each aging-out youth.

Now Brezan has a prospective family and an adult resource, both of which occurred only because of her initiative in contacting You Gotta Believe. Although there was no direct government involvement with Brezan's scenario, it is still critical in augmenting and monitoring the work of not-for-profits and faith-based institutions that administer child welfare services. So what if the government could take a step back and give the parenting responsibilities to somebody else?

The U.S. has countless foster children waiting for an adoptive family. Unfortunately, we do not have enough parents willing to provide a forever home or adoptive home for our adoptable foster children. If these children are not adopted and age out of foster care parentless, statistically a majority of them will end up recipients of public assistance or members of the incarcerated or homeless population—once again a great cost to taxpayers.

States have tried to address the needs of those aging out by teaching them how to live independently or by providing them temporary housing. However, despite the resources made available to these parentless youth, thousands will end up relying on public assistance or becoming homeless or incarcerated.

The State of Colorado realized that this formula of merely providing resources to aged-out foster children was inefficient, and that the kids could be better served by being placed with a permanent family while still in foster care. This realization prompted the state's dual-pronged effort that incorporated the faith-based community with a comprehensive assessment of how the state could better facilitate permanency.

Colorado began to address the need to find families by tapping into ready-made communities: faith-based institutions. By 2008, both the state and faith-based community were working in unison to identify permanent families for foster children who were freed for adoption. The churches' involvement is based on the concept that congregants would be willing to act upon a request from the pulpit. So faith leaders began integrating the message of permanency into their vision and sermons. Colorado faith leaders did this by organizing an effort called Project 1.27 after the Biblical passage in James 1:27, which implies that true religion is looking "after orphans and widows in their distress."

Through Project 1.27, the churches—in partnership with the state—built an infrastructure where they serve as liaisons between cooperative county and state agencies, and prospective and post-adoptive parents. Additionally, they not only recruit and train prospective parents but recruit volunteers from their congregations to serve as a support system for each permanent family.

According to media reports, the churches'

involvement substantially reduced the number of foster care children waiting for permanent homes from 875 in 2007 to 365 in 2010. Presently, Colorado only has 285 eligible children waiting for forever homes. Project 1.27 now serves as a model and resource for other states and cities that are interested in pursuing this model, which to date includes Washington, D.C. and Arizona.

Arizona's involvement in Project 1.27 rose from an effort to overhaul the State Child Protective Services Agency, including how it serves abused and foster children. After learning about the success of Colorado's Project 1.27, Governor Jan Brewer reached out to the ministers of Arizona's largest churches. According to one of those present at the meeting, Governor Brewer said the state couldn't parent foster children, because what they actually need is a committed parent to provide them a forever home, guidance and stability.

In response, the Arizona ministries partnered with the state and developed Arizona 1.27, affiliating churches that have integrated this vision into their sermons and developed services to support present and future forever families. In the fall of 2014, the Sun Valley Community Church held an awareness weekend and invited me to speak on a panel for five sermons at two different church campuses. The panel was moderated by the congregation's lead minister, Chad Moore, and consisted of three speakers that included a single adoptive mother of four, a father who promoted foster care adoption to his wife (they now have two toddlers), and me as a former foster child. Throughout the weekend, I was approached by numerous congregants who told me about their newly blended families that now include biological and adopted kids. Of course, just telling me did not prepare me for what I experienced on Sunday as the church members returned for my book signing. Families lined up to introduce me to their adoptive and foster kids, from infants to teens. The line was long, and the significance was powerful because it reinforced that integrating places of worship into the need for finding forever families, rather than just relying upon government, was working in this church in Arizona as it did throughout Colorado.

Being at Sun Valley Community Church reminded me of 15-year-old Davion O., a foster child who just last year stood before his fellow congregants and pleaded for a family that could "reach out and get me and love me until I die." Davion's mother was incarcerated when he was born and is now deceased. He has since been raised in foster care. "I just want people to know that it's hard to be a foster kid," he said. "People sometimes don't know how hard it is and how much we try to do good."

This courageous young man put into words what so many other foster children couldn't express—that they all deserve the unconditional love of a forever home. A family to surround them, even when they become adults. A parent who can become a grandparent to their own children. Davion has brought greater awareness to the need for forever families through his effort to publicly market himself for adoption.

Why did Davion do this? Because he knows what other older foster children know all too well: If they do not find a forever home, their destiny is solely up to them. They will sink or swim on their own. And that is a frightening and heavy burden for a parentless young adult to comprehend.

We should support and encourage all the Davions and Brezans among us, and let them know we understand how difficult life is for foster children. At the same time, we can show them we are ready to help them find the one thing that all children of any age really want: a family who will love them forever.

Gracie's Gift
Piper Punches

Our hands work in sync—up and down, up and down—the thin sliver of the quilting needles poking down and through the layers of fabric and then back up to repeat the process. The tops of my hands are knotty, my veins bulging up against my thinning skin. Hers are young and plump. They make me envious and taunt me with their youthful vigor. Mine shake too much from the medicine.

"Ouch!" The word hits my tongue sharply. A tiny drop of blood spreads out onto the cloth, turning the cotton candy colored fabric into a deep shade of red.

Gracelyn stands up quickly. Her chair clatters to the floor making Bernie, my 10-year-old Golden Retriever, momentarily glance up from his lazy slumber in the sunshine. "Let me get the peroxide. Maybe we can dab it out."

"Sit down, Gracie," I instruct. "There's a better way." I lower my lips to the fabric, and using the tip of my tongue, I lap at the blood stain until it disappears. Bernie looks at me curiously for a few seconds, then figures my lunacy isn't worth interrupting his nap time. But Gracelyn sits rooted in her chair. Her upper lip pulled back from her teeth and her eyes pinched together in disbelief.

"That is the grossest thing ever, GiGi," she exclaims.

"It worked. Didn't it?"

Gracelyn composes herself and shrugs. "It's still gross. Are you going to tell Mrs. Winters you licked her quilt?"

I cock my head and smile playfully. "You think I should?"

My granddaughter giggles, an 8-year-old giggle that is overflowing with playfulness and sprightliness. "No way. Our secret."

We work together in silence for another half hour. I glance at the clock and realize I should have started supper more than an hour ago, but I don't want to break the magic. Once I tell Gracelyn it is time to put the quilt away, the fragile fibers that connect us for this moment in time will instantly fray and break. She'll bound away from the quilting frame, grab her iPad and start Facetiming friends from school. She'll get lost in her television programs and pout when I tell her to start on her homework. It is the daily cycle of two different generations living together; me, so desperately trying to hold on to what is left, and her, ready to break free from my grip. Little does she know how soon that will be.

The tumor is inoperable.

"We can try to shrink it, Amelia," Allan told me in his office just a week earlier. He walked around his enormous desk, which seemed too exaggerated in such a tiny space. He pushed his glasses far up on the bridge of his nose. The lenses old, scratched from the time when he left them sitting in the sand at the beach, while we ignored the world and let the waves conceal our thoughtlessness and indiscretion. Was that really more than six years ago? He should have gotten rid of those glasses; bought new ones he could actually see out of instead of being cheap. Or maybe Allan wasn't being cheap. Maybe he, too, was holding on to the past.

What would his wife say? What did I care?

On that day, he was Dr. Patton, resting against the edge of the desk in front of me and talking about time. "If we can shrink the tumor with the medicine, maybe you'll have another good year."

So that was that. In a year or less, I would be dead. And what would become of Gracelyn?

As if reading my mind, Allan cleared his throat and broached the topic. "Have you told her yet?"

I shook my head and stared out the window. Why didn't he have a large window that overlooked the gardens? Shouldn't the primary oncologist at one of the most prestigious cancer centers on the Georgia coast be given a room with a view so his patients could catch a glimpse of Eden instead of the garbage truck pulling up to the dumpster when they were given their death sentence?

"Amelia," he scolded softly.

I turned back to face him. "What? How do I tell her? Would you want to have that conversation with an eight-year-old girl who has no one left in the world?"

"She has a father."

"No she doesn't," I said bitterly.

"It may be time to put aside your feelings and let him into her life."

"Gregory? Why would he be anything good for Gracie? He is the reason Lila is dead."

Allan stared down at his shoes. I followed his gaze. There were holes in the soles, and they needed to be polished. The nostalgia wafted out of my chest. Allan wasn't holding onto those glasses for sentiment. He really was just cheap. Accepting this renewed my sense of self, reminding me that counting on anyone in life was a waste of time.

"Merrie says her sister sees him at the First Baptist Church on Mansfield."

"Does she? Well, he must be preparing his résumé of good deeds for when he stands in front of those pearly white gates someday. But it doesn't bring Lila back."

"She says he sponsors several men at the AA meeting that meets in the basement."

"I think your wife should mind her own business, Allan. I know about alcoholics."

Just thinking about this last conversation with Allan makes me reach for the bottle of Jack Daniels that sits underneath the kitchen sink, lodged discreetly behind the Pine-Sol and Windex. I pause to listen for the sound of the television before pulling it out. The last time I opened it was six years ago—the day after Lila's funeral. Before then it sat undisturbed under the sink for nearly 12 years.

I should have gotten rid of it. Just two sips the day after I buried my only child didn't do anything to kill the pain, and I knew from past experience that chugging the entire bottle wouldn't help much either.

I learned how to hide liquor when I was around Gracie's age. First I hid it for my father when he came into my room after a night at See-Jay's Pub. "Take it, Amelia. Just put it behind your ponies on your shelf. This is our secret. Don't tell your mother." Like she didn't know.

Wives, husbands and children—you can't hide the stench of Jack Daniels from anyone. He permeated the skin and the hair, and oozed out of the pores. He stuck around like a shadow, refusing to leave even when the sun wandered behind a cloud. He was the love affair you wanted to end but couldn't resist. The only person you were fooling was yourself. But I hid the bottle for him anyway. I hid it in the toilet tank. I hid it underneath the loose floorboards on the sun porch. I hid it in the tire well of his mustard yellow 1960 Chevy Impala.

Two weeks after my 13th birthday, Mom left in the middle of the night. No note and no intentions of coming back. I hated her for leaving me with a man who cared more about his bottles of booze than making things right with his daughter. That's when I started finding better hiding places. Places for his booze that even he couldn't find. It wasn't long before it didn't matter if he found the hidden bottles because there would be nothing left. Not a drop. My daddy taught me well.

The sunlight warms my nose and makes it difficult for me to unwrap myself from the covers. My house is a couple of miles from the shoreline, but the ocean scent still drifts through the open window. Normally I welcome the sea's fragrance, but today all it does is make my stomach roll like fast and furious waves.

There is a soft knock on my bedroom door. "GiGi?"

I sit up and wrap the knotted pink and purple fleece throw around my upper body. It is the first blanket Gracie made. She was probably five or six at the time. I can't remember, but I smile, thankful I can remember how her little forehead wrinkled in concentration as she double-knotted each cut of fabric; the way her face lit up with satisfaction and confidence when she tied the last two pieces of fabric together and saw what her perseverance had created.

"GiGi," her tiny voice whispers against the door.

"Good morning, Gracie." I open the door and kiss

the top of her head. Her hair is raven black, her skin pale and translucent. We go through so much sunscreen to keep her skin from burning. The hair is a gift from her father, but her green eyes are entirely Lila's. "Are you hungry for breakfast?"

"I already ate breakfast. It's almost noon."

"What?"

"School called again."

"Shit!" I cover my mouth with the back of my hand. "I'm sorry, Gracie."

"It's OK. I'd rather be here with you. We can work on Mrs. Winter's quilt." Gracie smiled wide with a mouth full of missing teeth.

"No, it's not OK, Gracelyn. I'm sorry. You should be in school. Go get dressed. Quickly."

This is the fourth time in less than three weeks that I slept through my alarm. Hell, maybe I forgot to turn it on. I climb into my yoga pants and throw on a thin t-shirt. I know Allan is right. I need to make plans.

I run a comb through my thinning hair and avoid the mirror. I can't stand seeing the stranger who stares back at me. I look so old. Too old. Damn tumor is robbing me of everything: my memory, my appearance, my right to love and take care of Gracelyn like she is my own. People are starting to guess correctly that I am the grandmother instead of automatically assuming I am the mom, although I could be her mom. I had Lila when I was 16. Way too young to have a baby.

"If you aren't going to marry the bastard that knocked you up, then you may as well go to that clinic and take care of it," Daddy had said. His words were a tangled mess of long vowels and sloppy consonants. He tossed a pile of bills at me and staggered out of the room with Mr. Daniels swinging gleefully at his side, leaving me with a decision to make.

I never regretted one moment of being my daughter's

mother. It was hard, and her father wanted nothing to do with her or me. And, honestly, why would he? He was a foreman at the pulp mill, 10 years older than me with a wife and two children who looked like they were bred just to be on Christmas cards. The entirety of the situation was wrong, but having Lila felt right.

Pulling my hair into a pathetic ponytail, I walk into the living room. Gracelyn is sitting by the sliding door that leads out to the patio, petting Bernie and singing in his ear. I worried when she came to live with me that Bernie wouldn't be too happy to have a toddler around, a little person who required my constant attention. But that damn dog surprised me. He loved her like she was his own pup. It is good they have each other, but a dog can't take care of a child.

"Are you ready, Gracie?" I ask, grabbing my purse from alongside the couch.

Gracelyn sighed. "Oh, I guess. Can we work on the quilt when I get home?"

I nod. "If you don't have too much homework, OK, pickle?"

She smiled that toothless smile again. "OK, hamburger."

School doesn't give me too much grief over Gracie's tardiness. Although I did notice Emogene Landry, the school's lunch secretary, giving me a sideways glance as I shuffled out of the office after signing Gracie in. Well, Emogene can kiss my ass. Ever since high school she always thought she was better than me with her picture-perfect family, her straight-As and perfect attendance. She still thinks she's better than me, but I know her little secret. Hell, half of Brunswick knows her secret. They know that handsome, clever husband of hers may be an actuary by day for several financial firms near Savannah, but at night he unrolls his fishnet tights, pulls on a short skirt and wanders along the dodgier section of town. But what do I care? I can't waste what little time I have left worrying about anyone but Gracie and me.

Sliding into the driver's seat of my Corolla, I turn the key and make a left out of the parking lot. But instead of making my way toward the causeway to head home, I turn west on US 17. My memory may be slowly fading, but his address is etched on my temporal lobe: 575 Kingsway Drive.

I have been to the house at least 40 times since I was diagnosed. Each time I park a safe distance away, wearing a pair of tortoiseshell sunglasses and sometimes a tattered Braves ball cap. Not that I think Gregory would recognize me. We haven't spoken since the day of Lila's funeral. And the last time I saw him was when the parole board approved his early release from the correctional facility in Columbus. The board reduced his sentence from 10 years to less than two for good behavior and for his "exceptional remorse and intent to reconcile his past by helping other inmates achieve their own sobriety."

"What a load of horseshit," I told Allan when I walked out of the hearing, my heels echoing off the walls in the dark, narrow hallway.

"People can change, Amelia," Allan said as he put a comforting hand on the small of my back.

I looked at him, then looked at the ring on his left hand. It may have been 22 years later, but here I was still inserting myself into a relationship where I didn't belong with another man who couldn't fully be mine. "No, Allan. No, we really don't."

I ended things with him that night and vowed I would never let Gregory have his wish to reconcile with Gracie. Thank God he didn't fight me for her. He seemed to know his life's sentence was to be estranged from his daughter. But now things are different. Now, sitting in my car watching his house like an amateur PI, I realize maybe I did Gracie wrong. Maybe I did Lila wrong.

Was Gregory really a bad father? He drank too much at that party. So had Lila. The coroner's report found ample amounts of alcohol in her system too. They both got in the car and made the decision to drive home with Gracie, in the pouring rain, along a stretch of poorly lit highway that was notorious for being dangerous under the best conditions.

He said he didn't remember how the accident happened, only that he woke up and found Gracie lying in his lap, crying without a scratch on her, and Lila unmistakably dead, her body balancing grotesquely through the front windshield.

When the doorbell rang at three o'clock that morning, three days after Gracie's second birthday, I crept slowly to the entrance, taking a deep breath before peering through the diamond-shaped window in the center of the door. Good news doesn't knock on the door in the middle of the night. Good news is never delivered by a state trooper who crosses himself before the door is opened.

I could have lost them both. But by some miracle, a higher power allowed me to have Gracie. Now it was time to let her go.

I fiddle with my key ring. My legs feel like jelly, and I'm certain I can't do this, but then I realize there really isn't a choice. Unless I want Gracie to end up with strangers, bounced back and forth between one home and the next in the system, I have to do this.

I know he is there. I know he sleeps straight through the 10 o'clock hour and eats breakfast on his back porch at 11 o'clock every morning. This is because he works the second shift at the chemical processing plant. He doesn't have a girlfriend or anyone else in his life. In fact, if I am being honest, his life is lonely and pathetic. Exactly how mine would have been had I not been blessed with his daughter.

When I first started watching him, his pitiful existence justified my contempt. It served him right. Why should he get to have the life he wanted while Lila rotted in the Palmetto Cemetery? But as I returned to his street over and over again and confronted my own past, I realized it could have been me. How many times did I repeat the sins of my father? How many times did I get sloppy drunk when Lila was little? How many times did I drive her around town with the windows rolled down, sipping on that hot liquid from a Pepsi bottle?

When I approach the door, I hear the television humming. One of those ridiculous daytime talk shows that make you feel like you need to live off of supplements and false advertising, feeding you hope in a bottle. I guess we're all addicts in a way.

I press the doorbell and hold my breath. A flash of heat works its way from my chest up to my cheeks. Perspiration dampens my forehead. I used to joke with girlfriends saying I'd rather be dead than have to go through menopause. Who knew the universe had a sense of humor?

The door swings open, and Gregory stands in front of me, his massive six-foot-five frame bigger than the door's opening. He looks down at me, shock melting into satisfaction.

"Amelia," he says. "I was wondering how many times it would take before you finally decided to get out of that car."

Gracie and I quilt on Sundays now. First thing in the morning after she gets out of bed. She brings me a glass of orange juice, and I drink it in one gulp to wash down the tiny blue and white pills I take, meant to keep me on this earth a little while longer. Once I am up and dressed, we sit together in the living room with her Disney shows playing on the television and our fingers working together. We've got a rhythm, and it's comforting.

I know I won't be here to see the woman Gracelyn grows into, but I hope she remembers these times together. I try to teach her a little about life during our quilting sessions. Forget fairy tales. I keep it real. I tell her about her great-grandpa and how he didn't know how to fight the bad moods. I warn her there will be obstacles in life that may seem impossible to overcome and she may be tempted to push away the pain, but I remind her that one of the greatest gifts we have in life is to feel.

"Love. Pain. Joy. Sadness. Guilt. Life's a jumbled mess of feelings, Gracelyn. Don't be afraid to feel."

The evenings are when my symptoms are the worst. It is when the sun sets that I am reminded death is walking toward me. I hope it walks slowly, but some days when the pain is severe and it gets harder to remember the simplest things like what I had for breakfast or my middle name, I quietly urge it to hurry up.

Gregory takes Gracie in the evenings. The transition hasn't been as hard as I thought. He's a natural father. I know he carries guilt with him, and I can't say I've forgiven him entirely. It gives me a little satisfaction to see his shoulders slumped just a bit from the weight of his guilt, but for the most part, I'm learning to let go. I have to for Gracie's sake. She needs this man in her life. She needs a strong father. One who will guide her through life and help her grow into a beautiful, empowered woman. I only hope that wherever I go, I am allowed to witness her life.

I'm sitting on the sun porch when I hear the click of the front door. Usually Gracie comes running in at supercharged speed, jumping into my lap. Not tonight.

Tonight Gregory carries her in his arms.

"The fireworks wore her out," he says.

I smile. "I could see them from here. Just over the tops of the trees. Fireworks are one of Gracie's favorite things. Remember that."

He smiles. "I'm learning."

I stand up and stretch my sore limbs. "There's something I want to give you." I reach into the wooden chest near my chair and pull out the quilt. "We finished it this morning. I want you to keep it tucked away somewhere until she is older."

Gregory frowns at the colorful collection of fabric scraps sewn together to create a one-of-a-kind pattern. I run my hand over the motif quilting that is really quite impressive for a girl of Gracie's age. There are a few mistakes here and there, but it's pretty much flawless.

"I thought this was an order?"

"Oh goodness, no. I dissolved the business months ago. This was my gift to my granddaughter, a way for her to remember me and our special times together."

Gregory starts to cry, and I step down firmly on his toe. "Stop it. There'll be plenty of time for crying later. Right now let's just celebrate."

"Celebrate what?"

I look down at the quilt and realize the configuration of our lives is never perfect. That sometimes our colors clash and our patterns may be misshapen, but we do the best we can with what we have. "Life. It's short. We have to enjoy it while we can. Make sure Gracie knows this."

Gregory nods. I walk him to his car and watch him drive away. I don't know how much longer I have here, but I feel good about moving on. I may not have much to leave Gracie, but I hope she'll feel my love wrapped around her when she needs it the most.

Hope
Adria J. Cimino

The automatic doors slid open, and a burst of hot, humid air overwhelmed me. I'd been away so long that I'd forgotten the sensation. Imagining it in my mind, I had peeled off my layers of black in the airport restroom and stepped into light colors and flip flops. The sort of outfit I used to wear way back when.

In the airport parking lot, all was oddly still and quiet. Movement was absent. The constant flow of passersby bumping briefcases, taxis speeding along, street vendors shouting, drivers honking horns… This symphony of endless noise and activity that had enveloped me for the past eight years was nowhere to be found. In the city, I'd become so accustomed to this pulse that I no longer paid much attention to it. Yet now that it was gone, the silence choked me more than the heat.

Along with the high temperatures came the sun with a brightness I'd forgotten. I squinted behind my sunglasses and scowled. There were many cases of depression in these overly sunny places. The idea is, if you're already feeling kind of low, seeing the glaring sunshine just about every day of the year might push you lower. A friend from Australia once told me that. Sometimes, a gray day could be comforting. I probably should have thought about all of this before making a decision on a wild impulse.

But it was too late. My lease was up, and I'd left behind the life I'd known since reaching adulthood. Funny how in a period of a few hours, I could be here, in a different world. A stranger in this once familiar place. In a few hours, life could completely change.

I'd failed the bar. The news came earlier in the week, and I was still digesting it.

"Don't be discouraged, Cass. It's the most difficult one in the country! You'll ace it next time." Those were the words of my favorite professor, trying his best to boost my morale.

I didn't want morale-boosting or pity. I didn't want to cry on the shoulders of various friends and acquaintances.

Then there were the words of my father on the phone: "How could this be, Cassandra? You do realize you won't have a million chances? How could you let this happen?"

I didn't want scolding and criticism either. It wasn't as if I'd gone to the exam unprepared and purposely flunked. And it was a fine time for my father to start getting involved in my life after so many years of pushing me into the background. Since Mama died and he remarried. I was the reflection of her, the mother I didn't allow myself to remember. The coffee-colored skin and dark eyes set me apart from my white family. But I didn't want to think of any of them at the moment, even though I was back in their territory.

My best friend Marla distracted me from my thoughts. She was waving like a maniac. After our eyes met, she ran to me and folded me into a bear hug. We shoved my suitcase into the trunk of her car and drove toward our favorite watering hole.

We were the only customers at the beachfront café. The high season was over, and the locals were too busy with work and daily routines to spend time drinking along the seashore.

"I'm sorry about your exam, Cass," she said as we sat facing each other across a picnic table in the sand. A giant pair of sunglasses hid her blue eyes, but I didn't have to see them to know they were filled with compassion.

"Now what?" I replied. "That's the big question."

"You can take it again."

"I'm not sure if I want to." There. I'd said it. For the first time, I let out those words that scared me. After years of studying and sacrificing, of focusing on law and only law, I was questioning my own intentions. Was that the path I really wanted to take?

"Are you thinking of coming back here?" Marla asked.

I shook my head.

"Then why are you here now?"

"I needed to get away... and I didn't feel like planning a trip. So I chose the easiest option. Coming home."

But it was no longer home. That was the problem. When did it truly stop being home?

"You going there?" Marla asked. She knew the situation. She knew my father and stepmother didn't have a place in their life for me. I was too much of a reminder of my mother.

"I have no plans to see them."

The waiter brought us two giant iced teas, and I gazed for a moment at the gentle waves of turquoise water lapping at the shore. For years, the same small rowboat remained tied to a post at the water's edge.

Any normal person would find the setting idyllic and relaxing, but suddenly, to me it was simply a sore reminder of a less-than-happy past. Sorrow in paradise.

Marla dumped the contents of two pink packets into her drink and swirled the fake sugar around with her straw. I could tell she was contemplating the situation, trying to find a solution in her analytical mind.

"I remember your beautiful voice, Cass," she said, looking up at me.

I smirked. I knew what she was talking about. The performing arts program. The one we were both involved in until we parted ways and headed off to college.

"You're going to tell me I should be on Broadway," I said, rolling my eyes.

"No, I'm going to ask if you still sing."

"Once in a while… if the shower counts." And that was an exaggeration. The last time I sang in the shower was before my law school days.

"You do have an undergraduate degree in music."

I'd almost forgotten. Since entering law school, I'd closed the door to that part of my life. I'd actually closed the door to most things about my past. It was a miracle Marla and I remained best friends. The fact that she had come to visit me in the city several times, taking steps into my new world, had helped.

It wasn't as if music itself had been a negative part of my existence. As a matter of fact, it had been the one positive when I'd struggled through the loss of my mother. When family members returned to their own occupations, seemingly unaware of my suffering, I would sing. I would sing my sorrows and my joys.

"Cass, if you're doubting a career in law, why not return to what you loved most?"

"This isn't the time to make hasty decisions, Marla."

"A time like this is often the best moment for a hasty decision."

She was probably right. But I clung to the comfort of my stubbornness as if it were a cloak protecting me from instability and shook my head.

I would spend the night at Marla's condo on the beach. A new, neutral place. Unfamiliar. I truly was a stranger here. The clock struck midnight, and Marla was fast asleep. After our conversation, she was probably dreaming of ways to push me into taking charge of my future. I couldn't blame her. I might have done the same thing if I were in her situation and saw my sad-sack friend questioning the direction of her life.

I opened the sliding glass door, erasing the reflection of myself the dim lights had created. *Why do I have to look so much like my mother?* I thought as I meandered across the porch and into the sand. The fine crystals were cool on my bare feet.

Of course I saw this reflection of myself every day, yet thoughts of Mama only haunted me when I came back to this town. In my naïve mind, I thought this time would be different. I thought my worries about the bar and my future prospects would overshadow those old wounds. Maybe I'd come here as a test: If concerns about those concrete problems could wipe away most thoughts of Mama, I was over it. Well, if that was the case, I'd failed my second test in a week.

Mama left when I was 6 years old. She told me she was going to the hospital for treatment so she would be well again, so we could run around the yard together and swim in the pool. But she never came back. When Dad told me the news, I hardly listened. I was already inventing an outcome that wasn't as painful: Mama was in some sort of rehabilitation. She would be back once she was cured. I hung onto this scenario for a long while. Even after Dad remarried two years later.

When Dad and Lauren did their own thing, when they were happy and I was sad, I said to myself: Soon, Mama will be back, and everything will be OK. Mama and I can move away together. And Dad and Lauren won't be bothered any more with people saying in surprise, "*You're* Cassandra's parents?" They would be better off without me—and I would be better off without them.

But things didn't work out that way. I eventually let go of the childish hope of Mama returning. I'd realized Dad had told me the truth. Slowly but surely, I'd become an orphan. And this town was no longer my home.

Moonlight illuminated the dark waves, and white foam crashed along the shore. A sound that should have been soothing. How many people buy CDs of this kind of thing just to get to sleep? And there I was, crying my eyes out over the loss of Mama 20 years ago.

I borrowed Marla's car. Dad and Lauren would both be at work, and I still had keys to the house. I decided I couldn't come back to this town any time soon. Therefore, I had to build up my courage, return to my old room and collect belongings I might need in the near future.

I couldn't imagine much being left behind since I cleared out my room when I left for college, but it would be ridiculous to come this far and not do a final check.

The house was still and quiet, like everything else around here. My heart was beating a mile a minute as I turned my key in the lock. As if I were a burglar rather than a girl who used to live here. Inside, the scent of Dad's woodsy cologne mixed with the sharp oriental scent of Lauren's perfume. I remembered when Mama's gardenia fragrance permeated the air, and then I pushed the thought out of my mind. I was here on a mission.

Quickly, I glanced around. Nothing had changed. The same white furnishings, the same gray carpet, the same clutter of flower paintings Lauren had tacked on the walls. I made my way down the hall to my bedroom. And here, there was a transformation. They had turned it into a sitting room. The final detail to eliminate my presence. How many hours had I spent in that room feeling small and invisible?

We used to be happy a long time ago. When Mama was healthy and the three of us would walk along the beach or play board games on rainy days. My parents were in love with each other and loved me. When Mama left for the hospital that last time, my father changed. Well before Lauren came into the picture, he pushed me aside. I remembered curling up in my bed, talking to Mama as if she were right next to me, then crying myself to sleep. Many, many nights. I could still see my own image, fragile and alone. Dad refused to return to Martinique, where he had met Mama and where her brothers and sisters still lived. After years of letters, we lost touch, and I lost hope. If they really cared about me, wouldn't they have found a way to see me?

I took a deep breath and pushed the memories away.

I opened the closet, and my eyes traveled from end to end, searching for any remnant of my presence here. In the corner, I found a stack of papers from high school. After flipping through the pages, I shoved them back on the shelf. It was then that a word caught my eye. On a box half hidden by the clothes Lauren used to wear before the diet shaved off 50 pounds.

Hope. Mama's name.

With trembling hands, I lifted the lid and waded through a bunch of withered hospital bills. My fingers touched something hard. A notebook. I opened it and recognized Mama's handwriting. There was an inscription on the first page: To Cassandra. My whole body was shaking by that point. I stuffed the book into my handbag, hastily returned everything to its place and hurried out the door.

The city, the bar, the movement, the noise: All of that seemed to be part of my life long ago. It was as if in another lifetime, as a matter of fact. Somehow, my childhood in this small coastal town and the loss of my mother had become my reality. The distant past was my present. And I still had no idea about my future.

I ran to that spot on the beach where Mama and I would sit and talk. I'd left Marla with the car keys and an awkward excuse about needing time alone. She knew something was up but was a good enough friend to give me space.

My fingers raced through those pages of tales about my silly games and adventures, my joys and heartaches, and my accomplishments and disappointments. I could no longer remember my mother's voice, yet somehow it was speaking to me as I turned each page, showing someone did indeed care about me one day and continued to care beyond this life. Although Mama didn't say much about herself, through her words, I was getting to know her from my perspective as an adult.

As her illness gained ground, she continued to write. Selflessly. About me. Singing in the choir, learning how to read, falling off my bike but refusing to cry, swimming in Martinique. On that last trip. The memory came back to me as I read her words.

I pieced the story together. Mama's family didn't like my father... because he accepted his family's behavior. Dad's family rejected Mama—and rejected me. Right then and there, I was that little girl chewing one of

Grandma's cod fritters and noticing the looks they exchanged, Grandma and Dad. It was a question of race. As much as I knew that deep down all of my life, it hit me like a slap. It was one thing to have a stranger give you a funny look when he saw you with your white father. It was another thing to have the hatred in your own family.

Grandma was gone the same year as Mama. But there were aunts, uncles, cousins. Mama wrote about how they loved me, but it was "difficult" for them to visit us. And she was too weak to make another trip to Martinique. That entire part of my existence disappeared with Mama.

I turned to the last page of the notebook, skipping many in between. Mama's final words made up the message I needed to hear:

Today, I told you I was going to the hospital but soon would be home. It was a lie, my darling, only to protect you. But I realize I've only delayed the pain and created false hopes. I'm sorry, my daughter, for leaving you when what I want most is to be by your side. I want you to know I put up a battle, and I did so for you. I want you to know that in the six years I spent with you on this earth, in spite of my illness, you have made me happier than I could ever imagine. I am proud of you, and I am proud of the woman I'm certain you will become. I hope I have left you with enough love, faith and courage to follow your heart and believe in yourself. That would be my victory. I hope that as you face any challenge, you will remember the human spirit is a lot stronger than we often give it credit for. And I hope you know I will be forever in your heart, loving you.

Instead of crying, I started to sing. The voice I'd forgotten hadn't disappeared. Softly, gently, the melody spilled out with much more emotion than my tears could ever bring. It rose above the ocean and into the sky, in acknowledgement of those words written long ago. I held the notebook against my chest and closed my eyes.

The sun had set by the time I wandered back to Marla's condo. She was tossing a salad big enough for at least four, but I didn't worry about having to put on a brave face for visitors. Marla always prepared twice as much food as was necessary.

"Let me help with something," I said, eager for a distraction.

"You're my guest," she said, smiling and shaking her head. "After the rough week you had, you deserve a break…"

"I'd rather keep busy."

"You want to cook together, like we used to?"

"It's been too long." This time I smiled. My first real smile since I'd arrived.

Marla pushed a head of broccoli in my direction and turned up the heat under a pan.

"Let's stir fry!" she said.

So we did. As if everything was normal. As if I hadn't failed the bar, hadn't left the city for good, hadn't cried about the past. As if I'd simply come here on vacation to resume the friendship we had when we were 18.

We sat on the patio, where the scent of salty air perfumed our plates, and the sound of the ocean offered constant background music.

We savored our chicken and vegetables, toasted with glasses of white wine and saved room for raspberry sorbet. We talked about Marla's accounting job, my last internship at a big law firm, and the latest books we'd read and films we'd seen. Marla talked about her breakup with Jay and his incessant pleas to win her back. I told her to reconsider as I'd done after their earlier breakups.

"You're perfect together! Why can't you see it?"

She smirked and let out a sigh.

And then, as we reached the bottom of the wine bottle, Marla squinted and studied me. I knew it was coming. She wouldn't let me off the hook that easily.

"Cass, if you're not ready to make a decision about your future, that's OK. How about if you stay with me for a while? You're more than welcome, you know. I've got plenty of room!" She reached across the table and squeezed my hand. "Just have your stuff shipped from New York…"

In a split second, my city life, my beach-town life and everything in between flashed before my eyes. The grand finale was this afternoon holding Mama's notebook in my hands and my voice breaking free. As I sat there facing Marla, yet seeing myself, I knew. All of a sudden, I knew.

"I'm leaving tomorrow," I said. "Finally, I have a destination."

I slept like a log for the first time in months and woke up to the cry of seagulls. I was feeling more comfortable in this place than I'd felt in years, and yet it was time to leave. Marla didn't try to discourage me. She heard me singing in the shower and saw the sparkle in my eyes. I called the airport to reserve my ticket, and for once, there wasn't a problem or delay.

And a few hours later, I was on my way to that island of my past with the hope my mother had brought to my heart.

About the Authors

Allison Hiltz, Preface

Allison Hiltz runs the award-winning book blog, The Book Wheel, and is the founder of the international blog roundup event, #30Authors. Allison's site has received numerous awards and mentions from literary sites and organizations. Whether she is reading, blogging, studying or working, Allison probably has a cup of coffee in her hand. She lives in the Denver Metro Area with her husband and two rescue dogs, where she is finishing up her Master of Public Policy degree at the University of Denver. She plans to launch her career in policy, while blogging during every other minute she has (and a few she doesn't). Catch up with Allison at TheBookWheelBlog.com.

Regina Calcaterra, "A Forever Home"

Regina's memoir *Etched in Sand* is a *New York Times* and *Wall Street Journal* best seller. It was selected for One Book/One College reads and integrated into college and high school curriculums. For the past 26 years, Regina has spent her policy, managerial and legal career in both the private and public sectors. She is presently an attorney working for the State of New York. She proudly serves as board vice president to You Gotta Believe, an organization that works toward finding older foster children forever homes. Regina lives with her companion, Todd Ciaravino, and their two cocker spaniels, Maggie and Oscar. Check out Regina's work at ReginaCalcaterra.com.

Stephanie Carroll, "Forget Me Not"

As a reporter and community editor, Stephanie Carroll earned first place awards from the National Newspaper Association and from the Nevada Press Association. She holds degrees in history and social science, and graduated with honors. Her dark and magical style, found in *A White Room*, is inspired by the classic authors Charlotte Perkins Gilman (*The Yellow Wallpaper*), Frances Hodgson Burnett (*The Secret Garden*) and Emily Bronte (*Wuthering Heights*). Stephanie lives in California, where her husband was originally stationed with the U.S. Navy and where she founded Unhinged & Empowered, an inspiring and empowering blog for Navy wives, girlfriends and significant others. Learn more about Stephanie's writing at StephanieCarroll.net.

Adria J. Cimino, "Hope"

Adria J. Cimino is the author of novels *Paris, Rue des Martyrs* and *Close to Destiny*, a contributor to anthology *That's Paris* and co-founder of indie publishing house Velvet Morning Press. Prior to jumping into the publishing world full time, she spent more than a decade as a journalist at news organizations including The AP and Bloomberg News. In addition to writing fiction and discovering new authors, Adria writes about her real-life adventures at AdriaInParis.blogspot.com. You can learn more about Adria and her work at AJCimino.com.

Maureen Foley, "Bound by Water"

Maureen Foley is a writer, teacher and artist who lives on an avocado ranch by the sea with her family. Her writing has appeared in *The New York Times, Caesura, Santa Barbara Magazine* and *Wired,* as well as in numerous literary journals. Her novella, *Women Float,* is a coming-of-age story set in Carpinteria, California, and was published in June 2013 by the Chicago Center for Literature and Photography. In 2013, she started Red Hen Cannery, a small-batch artisanal jam company. You'll find more about Maureen at MaureenFoley.com.

Lizzie Harwood, "How to Raise Cats in a Paris Apartment"

Lizzie Harwood's love of her home country, New Zealand, spills over into her writing, as evidenced by the vibrant—and sometimes charmingly quirky—stories she tells. That isn't to say she doesn't adore her adopted country, France, where she currently resides with her husband and two children. She writes with a passion inspired by living and traveling around the world. Lizzie's short story collection, *Triumph: Collected Stories of Gone Girls and Complicated Women,* was published in February 2015. When she isn't writing, she's neck-deep in editing at EditorDeluxe.com.

J.J. Hensley, "Four Days Forever"

J.J. Hensley is a former police officer and Special Agent with the U.S. Secret Service who has drawn upon his experiences in law enforcement to write stories full of suspense and insight. J.J., who is originally from Huntington, WV, graduated from Penn State University with a B.S. in Administration of Justice and has an M.S. degree in Criminal Justice Administration from Columbia Southern University. He is currently a training supervisor with the U.S. Office of Personnel Management and lives with his beautiful wife, daughter and two dogs near Pittsburgh, PA. His first novel, *Resolve*, was named one of the Best Books of 2013 by *Suspense Magazine* and was a finalist for Best First Novel by the International Thriller Writers organization. Learn more about J.J. at Hensley-Books.com.

Kristopher Jansma, "The Uraniums"

Kristopher Jansma is the winner of the 2014 Sherwood Anderson Award for Fiction. His first novel, *The Unchangeable Spots of Leopards*, received an Honorable Mention for the 2014 PEN/Hemingway Award and was longlisted for the Andrew Carnegie Medal for Excellence and the Flaherty-Dunnan Debut Novel Prize. His second novel, *What Can Go Wrong*, will be published in 2016. He has written for *The New York Times*, *Johns Hopkins Magazine*, *Slice Magazine*, *The Believer*, *Adult Magazine* and *Blue Mesa Review*. He is a graduate of the Writing Seminars program at Johns Hopkins University and received his MFA in Fiction at Columbia University. He is a graduate lecturer at Sarah Lawrence College and assistant professor at SUNY New Paltz College. You'll find more about Kristopher at KristopherJansma.com.

Vicki Lesage, "Apfelstrudel"

Vicki Lesage proves daily that raising French kids isn't as easy as the hype lets on. In her three minutes of spare time per week, she writes, sips bubbly and prepares for the impending zombie apocalypse. She lives in Paris with her French husband, rambunctious son and charming daughter, all of whom mercifully don't laugh when she says "au revoir." She penned *Confessions of a Paris Party Girl* and #1 Amazon Best Seller *Confessions of a Paris Potty Trainer*, contributed to anthology *That's Paris* and co-founded indie publishing house Velvet Morning Press. She writes about the ups and downs of life in the City of Light at VickiLesage.com.

Jenny Milchman, "Two Kinds of Legacy"

Jenny Milchman is a suspense writer from New York, who lived for seven months on the road with her family on what Shelf Awareness called "the world's longest book tour." Jenny's debut novel, *Cover of Snow*, earned starred reviews from *Publishers Weekly* and *Booklist*, as well as praise from *The New York Times*, *San Francisco Journal of Books* and The AP. It won the Mary Higgins Clark Award for best suspense novel of 2013. *Ruin Falls* was published in 2014 to starred reviews from *Booklist* and *Library Journal*, and chosen as a 10 Best of 2014 by *Suspense Magazine*. Her third novel, *As Night Falls*, will be published in 2015. Jenny's short fiction has appeared in *Ellery Queen Mystery Magazine*, multiple anthologies and online. Jenny is vice president of author programming for International Thriller Writers, founder of Take Your Child to a Bookstore Day, and teaches writing and publishing for New York Writers Workshop. Learn more about Jenny at JennyMilchman.com.

Piper Punches, "Gracie's Gift"

Piper Punches is a habitual truth-bender turned novelist who describes her writing as "human interest fiction." Her debut novel, *The Waiting Room*, and her second published work, the novella *Missing Girl*, are both Amazon Top 10 Best Sellers. Piper isn't afraid to reach deep into your soul and bring injustices front and center. Piper aspires to develop smart fiction that entertains and educates. Find out more about Piper at PiperPunches.com.

Didier Quémener, "Letters of the Night (Adeline and Augustin)"

Executive chef, private chef, food and wine consultant... Lived in the U.S., based in Paris: does not wear a beret but eats freshly baked bread every day. Cooked his first meal at age seven, graduated from the Sorbonne, worked as a photographer and finally came back to the kitchen where it all started. Didier is French and American, therefore obnoxious, a wine snob and speaks loudly! When Didier is not cooking, he's writing. When he's not writing, he's playing golf. When he is not playing golf, he's dreaming of being an orchestra conductor, or a guitar player, or... Back to reality: A husband, a father and a foodie! Didier contributed to anthologies *Mystery in Mind* and *That's Paris* and is working on a full-length food and wine memoir. You can find him at ChefQParis.com and FoodMe.fr.

Marissa Stapley, "The Monument"

Marissa Stapley is a National Magazine Award nominated writer who has contributed to many publications, including *Globe and Mail*, *National Post* and *Elle*. Her debut novel, *Mating for Life*, is a Canadian bestseller. She lives in Toronto with her husband and two children, where she is working on a new novel and teaching creative writing at the University of Toronto. Learn more about Marissa's work at MarissaStapley.com.

David Whitehouse, "Nagasaki"

David Whitehouse finds non-fiction easier and less revealing than fiction. He has written a book on the question of Rwandan genocide suspects in France, *In Search of Rwanda's Génocidaires: French Justice and the Lost Decades*. He was the ghostwriter for the autobiography of long-time Cambodia opposition leader Sam Rainsy, *We Didn't Start the Fire: My Struggle for Democracy in Cambodia*.

Paula Young Lee, "Sonny's Wall"

Paula Young Lee is the author of numerous books on the cultural history of meat, including *Meat, Modernity, and the Rise of the Slaughterhouse*, *Game: A Global History* and *Deer Hunting in Paris: A Memoir of God, Guns, and Game Meat* (winner of the 2014 Lowell Thomas Award of the Society of American Travel Writers). She holds a doctorate from the University of Chicago and contributes regularly to venues such as Salon.com, Dame.com, The Blot.com and The Conversation (UK). Her second memoir, in-progress, is *The Swamp Yankee Chronicles*, about rural life in Maine.

Acknowledgements

Velvet Morning Press would like to thank Allison Hiltz of The Book Wheel website for helping us turn her 30 Authors blogging event into this legacy-themed anthology. And we as authors and publishers thank the book blogging community for reading our book and writing about it. We appreciate your support!

A big thank you to all of the contributors who shared their work and their time with us, offering the gift of beautiful words. It was wonderful to see how each of you took the idea of legacy and made it your own. We hope your stories will delight readers just as much as they delighted us as we assembled this anthology.

As always, a thank you to Ellen Meyer, who makes all of the Velvet Morning Press books look lovely.

And finally, thank you, readers, for making reading your legacy.

About Velvet Morning Press

Velvet Morning Press is a boutique publishing house that discovers new authors and launches their careers. VMP publishes fiction in a variety of categories, short story anthologies and special projects involving new and established authors.

Adria J. Cimino and Vicki Lesage are the women behind VMP. Both authors themselves, Vicki and Adria use their experience in writing, editing and marketing to bring the work of other writers to bookshelves. VMP's anthologies include *Legacy* and *That's Paris*.

If you enjoyed this collection of legacy stories, please consider leaving a review on Amazon—even just a few sentences!

Want more? Get *Recipes and Reads* for free! Simply join Velvet Morning Press's new release mailing list: http://bit.ly/vmp-news.

A taste of the good life in...
Recipes and Reads

You know that feeling you get after you turn the last page of a great book? It's similar to the feeling you get after enjoying a delicious meal. Satiated. Pleased. Relaxed. Yet... eager for the next slice of goodness!

So, as publishers, readers and food-lovers, we decided to pair our favorite indulgences into this appetizing guide of great reads and great recipes.

Get it for free! Join the Velvet Morning Press new release mailing list and we'll send you a free ecopy of *Recipes and Reads*: http://bit.ly/vmp-news.

Additional Titles by Velvet Morning Press

That's Paris: An Anthology of Life, Love and Sarcasm in Paris, featuring a foreword by Stephen Clarke
Multi-Author Short Story Collection

If you've ever traveled to Paris, lived in the City of Light or dreamed of setting foot on its cobblestoned streets, you'll enjoy escaping into this collection of stories about France's famed capital. From culinary treats (and catastrophes) to swoon-worthy romantic encounters (and heartbreaking mishaps), this anthology takes you on a journey through one of the most famous cities in the world.

Survival of the Ginnest, by Aimee Horton
Chick Lit/Mom Lit

Meet Dottie Harris. Dottie spent her late 20s working her way up the career ladder, but things are about to change. In this modern-day diary, Dottie, after announcing her pregnancy, turns to social networking to build a new social life. She quickly begins to rely on it—along with gin—as a way to reach out and remind herself of the funny side of the frustrations of motherhood.

Entanglement, by Katie Rose Guest Pryal
Women's Fiction

Awkward 21-year-old Greta Donovan, the fiercely intelligent daughter of a philandering professor, doesn't relate to people nearly as well as she relates to facts and figures. While Greta gets quarks and string theory, she hasn't a clue where men are concerned. She moves to L.A. with her best friend Daphne, a troubled girl with an abusive past. Daphne betrays Greta while throwing a dangerous man in her path. Can Greta survive? Can she forgive?

Paris, Rue des Martyrs, by Adria J. Cimino
Literary Fiction

Some encounters make a difference. Four strangers in Paris. Each one is on a quest: to uncover a family secret, to grasp a new chance at love, to repair mistakes of the past. Four stories entwine, four quests become one, as their paths cross amid the beauty, squalor, animation and desolation of a street in Paris, the rue des Martyrs.

Close to Destiny, by Adria J. Cimino
Contemporary Fiction/Magical Realism

A story of the role of destiny in life... and of righting the wrongs of the past. Kat, a young woman facing inner demons, is plagued by strange encounters at a London hotel. The experiences make her question her own notion of reality and the power she holds over her own destiny.

Petite Confessions, by Vicki Lesage
Humor/Memoir

From champagne bottles to baby bottles, this memoirette offers a humorous look at an American mom's decade in Paris. Party Girl Vicki moved to the City of Light hoping to drink her fill of wine and fall in love. She accomplished her goal but encountered many bumps along the way: romantic encounters gone awry, absurd French bureaucracy threatening her sanity, and two adorable but impossibly energetic kids keeping her on her toes. You'll laugh, you'll cry, you'll want to open another bottle of wine.

Confessions of a Paris Party Girl, by Vicki Lesage
Humor/Memoir

Wine, romance and French bureaucracy—the ups and downs of an American's life in Paris. Full of sass, shamefully honest admissions and situations that seem too absurd to be true, you'll feel as if you're stumbling along the cobblestones with Vicki. Will she find love? Will she learn to consume reasonable amounts of alcohol? Will the French administration ever cut her a break?

Confessions of a Paris Potty Trainer, by Vicki Lesage
Humor/Memoir

Diapers, tantrums and French bureaucracy—the crazy life of an American mom in Paris. Think French parenting is easy? Think again! Former party girl Vicki trades wine bottles for baby bottles, as this sassy mommy of two navigates the beautiful, yet infuriating, city of

Paris. This humorous memoir will have you laughing, crying, and wiping up drool right alongside Vicki as she and her ever-patient French husband raise two children in the City of Light.

Made in the USA
Charleston, SC
23 June 2016